Strike the Harp!

Strike the Harp!

American Christmas Stories

Owen Parry

wm

William Morrow

An Imprint of HarperCollins*Publishers*

HarperCollins books may be purchased for educational, business, or sales promotional use. For information please write: Special Markets Department, HarperCollins Publishers Inc., 10 East 53rd Street, New York, NY 10022.

FIRST EDITION

Designed by Fearn Cutler de Vicq

Printed on acid-free paper

Library of Congress Cataloging-in-Publication Data

Parry, Owen.
      Strike the harp! : American Christmas stories / Owen Parry.— 1st ed.
          p. cm.
      Contents: Coal & iron—We kings—Appearances—Herod—How Jimmy Mulvaney astonished the world for Christmas—In every inn—The Christmas Joe—The day after Christmas—The lie of the land—On Christmas night.
      ISBN 0-06-057236-1 (alk. paper)
      1. Christmas stories, American. I. Title.
PS3566.E7559S75 2004
813'.54—dc22   2004044951

04 05 06 07 08 WBC/RRD 10 9 8 7 6 5 4 3 2 1

To Maisie,
who had to clean up the Christmas-morning mess

Contents

Strike the Harp!

Coal & Iron

Christmas Eve, 1887

Captain Davies recoiled from the hag. As hard as the miners' lot had become, he never had thought to hear such words from a woman's lips. The lump of coal in her up raised hand seemed less of a threat to order than her language.

"Ye filthy, low taffy" was the kindest thing she said. "Ye'd let the babes freeze up and die, and call yourself a Christian all the while. Ye haven't the heart of a Herod."

Her slight arm drifted lower as she spoke, but when she had done with spitting words, she renewed her threat by raising the lump again: a piece of coal the size of a fist in a woman's naked hand. The hatred scorching her eyes might have melted the crust of snow from the culm banks and thawed the ice that covered the blackened creek.

"That is enough now, Mrs. O'Kane," Davies said in a voice that was firm but not loud. "Go home with you. That is enough."

"Enough?" The rage in the word was startling. "Ye'll know it well when *we*'ve had enough, ye and every Coal & Iron copper in the valley." But the strength in her arm, if not in her heart, had already begun to fail. The lump of coal sank earthward.

Her anger collapsed in despair. She added only, "The lads'll let the likes o' ye know when they've had enough. That they will. Wait and see, ye black-hearted, black-faced Welshman."

For a few startling moments, her fury had risen to grandeur. But she lacked the animal vigor to sustain it. Davies knew well that Mary O'Kane was the sort who would crimp her own portion to lay a bit more mash on a grandchild's plate, and even the bundle of rags wrapped around her could not give bulk to her form. She became a ravaged old woman again, a slumped creature in a man's overcoat whose ragged hem picked up the slush as she turned and made her way off along the railroad ties.

Harris, the new man, had come up behind her and the children, fingering his truncheon. As the crone shuffled past, he said in a voice too loud, "And don't let me see that mug of yours on company property again. We got cells for women, too, don't think we don't."

The old woman muttered into her scarf, waving a lowered hand for her tribe to follow her. The families sent the very old and the very young to walk the railbed now, to collect any coal that had fallen from the cars. It long had been a privilege allowed the miners' families. But no more. Not since the strike dragged on and the company hardened. And the miners—so proud so recently—bent to their wives' complaints, letting grandmothers and children sneak out to gather what they could between patrols. Hoping to find mercy where there was none.

"That's right," Harris told her, digging his thumbs into the belt that gathered in his greatcoat. "Get out of here, you old witch."

Captain Davies regretted his subordinate's words almost as deeply as he regretted the man himself. The newest addition to his force had been chosen by his superiors, not by Davies. Harris was a mongrel sort of man, English by his name, American-born by his tone. He was a bully, not suited to the work of a proper policeman.

The strike had changed so many things. No stoppage in decades had gone on so long. Misled by dreamers, the miners had convinced themselves that the coal companies all through the anthracite fields would have to give in before Christmas, as the winter demanded coal for the nation's stoves, for factory furnaces and metropolitan boilers. But the strike had been anticipated by their masters. The yards in Philadelphia and New York had been overstocked that summer, and the coal was piled so high on the Baltimore docks that it looked like black mountains rising from the sea.

Such matters had not been confided to the captain, of course. He was not placed high enough to be invited to the councils held in the fine offices in Pottsville or Reading or Philadelphia. Davies knew these things because it was his job to listen to all men, at all times. And his uniform, so prominent in the lives of the poor, gave him a measure of invisibility with the colliery lords who came to visit the works, as well as with the superintendents, the countinghouse men, and the lawyers. They did not hesitate to speak frankly in the presence of the loyal Captain Davies.

According to the labor organizers, who came from beyond the valley, the strike was to have ended before Christmas, in a victory for the men who dug the coal. Now it was Christmas Eve, with the heavens gray and the first snow already dirty in the yards. The evictions had begun, the cruelest work that David Davies had ever been ordered to do. In better years, the rare turning out of a family was meant to rid the patch or the town above it of violent drunkards or laborers who worked carelessly and put good men at risk down in the galleries. But since Thanksgiving, the captain had been directed to flush out families he had known most of his life, the wives and children of men whose work had never come into question. Some had spoken too loudly at the wrong times, while others had grown too old to be of use. The company was culling the wheat from the chaff and wasting no time in doing it.

Davies consoled himself that the law was the law, that private property was private property, and that company regulations had to be enforced to keep the world from chaos. But he found his duties harder every day.

And the families not yet evicted from their shanties survived on potatoes and barrels of cabbage dragged over the hill from Tamaqua by the benevolent association. Poverty had never been a stranger to the valley. But there had been work for the willing, and hunger had been rare, even if the lads were not treated to cakes and ale every evening.

Now even the skilled miners had emptied their tin boxes of their savings, and the laborers who did the navvy work down the shaft or in the colliery looked as gaunt as the birches climbing the waste banks, white and bare and shivering. Households sold what they could, even their Sunday finery. Captain Davies knew that when certain women appeared in the mud of the lanes, their husbands would be at home by dormant hearths, since the family had but one winter coat left between them. Man and wife could not go outside together.

Thinned to snapping, the children scratched in their rags. Even the Irish saloons were shuttered more often than they were open.

Davies watched the woman's crooked back fade down the line toward the bridge that led to the company houses. The children following her gathered their shoulders down toward their chests, already defeated, practicing the posture that would haunt them all their days.

"Bums," Harris said, taking up a chesty stance beside the captain. "No-good, lazy bums, them Irish. And the Hunkies we got coming in are worse."

Davies looked at the man, and he did not like what he saw. Harris was a good six inches and a bad sixty pounds greater in size, and younger by twenty years, but Davies sensed that the fellow's courage was as brittle as ice grown over a water trough. He could be beaten by any man with a will. Harris had complained, more than once, that Davies restricted his men to carrying billy clubs, while the Coal & Iron Police at the other collieries had already drawn their Winchesters from the armories.

"We are not 'other collieries,'" Davies had told him. "And you will do well to remember it, Mr. Harris. And you will not forget to call me 'sir,' thank you."

"Well, they're nothing but Mollie Maguires, every one of them Irish. *Sir*." The new man had given Davies a coward's glance, measuring how much would be tolerated. "They won't be happy 'til somebody's laying dead. We ought to be carrying Winchesters, like the boys at Number Seven."

But there would be no rifles issued, not if Davies could help it. Nor would the regulation Colts be handed out, despite the rumors of trouble. Davies never had tolerated brass knuckles or even rudeness among his subordinates. Not that it had gained him much affection. His lot in life was that of a company policeman, and such were disliked even in the best of times.

But Davies had always regarded himself as an honest man, simply upholding the law. And when the law fell short, his temperament could settle for regulations. His youth had been shaped by war, when his regiment, the 48th, dug the mine at Petersburg, only to gape in horror at the chaos that followed their work.

Captain David Davies hated chaos. Or even the slightest disorder. His life had convinced him that men were unruly by nature and wanted fair-minded discipline. Either that of a printed code or, better still, that of the chapel. A man's life should run as smoothly in its tracks as a well-tended locomotive, and his direction should be as unwavering.

He had kept good order without too heavy a hand. In rising to his captaincy, he did not believe that he had ever mistreated a single man or even a vagrant hound. At least not until this strike. And if he could never be loved because of his position, he always had believed himself respected. Until now. Until that afternoon, in fact, the Christmas Eve when Mary O'Kane had turned her curses upon him.

The small, black figures of the coal thieves crossed the bridge and faded into the shanties. Davies sighed. A final promotion had been hinted to him, a grand lifting out of the valley to the company's central office, as soon as the strike was over. Once he would have scorned the thought of sitting behind a desk all day, away from the daily run of men and women, separated from the life of it all. But now he longed for the new position, for the chance to avoid forever after the weeping and the curses, the terrified look of children put from their homes, their fear born of the helplessness they read in their parents' faces, the paralysis of men made weak by law and the despair of women whose lives were summed by a pile of shabby possessions cast into the street.

"Look you, Mr. Harris," Davies said to his subordinate. He had decided to try one more time to get through to the man. "Tell me what you see there, would you do that?"

Harris roiled his shoulders like a boxer sizing up an opponent. "An old mick witch . . . and a pack of little mick monkeys. Who don't belong in this country in the first place."

"That is not what I mean, Mr. Harris. What do you see farther on, man? Among the houses? Anything at all?"

The policeman stared, then squinted. Davies could feel the man's suspicion. Of a test, a trap.

"I don't see one damned thing. Sir."

"That is correct, Mr. Harris. Because there is nothing to see. Unless it is the absence of a thing."

Harris looked at the captain, not at the village. The policeman's face said, "I don't like riddles, and I don't like you."

"Confused, is it?" Davies said in the calm voice he rarely ruptured. "But you are not from our valley, then. Look you, Mr. Harris. Often, it is what a man does *not* see that should trouble him." He stared up into the face of his subordinate—a face that could not have been better selected to raise a miner's hackles at first sight. "How many chimneys are smoking among the houses there?"

The policeman squinted again. "It's hard to see."

"It is hard to see because hardly a one is smoking. The hearths are cold, Mr. Harris. And the stoves are colder still. And that is why they are coming for the coal, see."

The policeman answered with a grimace that said, "Any fool could have told you that."

The captain tried another tack. "How old would you judge I am?"

Harris sized him up. "Fifty, maybe."

Davies nodded. "Well, that is close enough. And how old would you judge Mrs. O'Kane to be? The woman we have only chased away?"

Harris shrugged. "Dunno. Sixty-five? Seventy?"

"She is younger than me. By two or three years. It is a hard life they have, see."

But Davies had wasted his breath. He saw that he had only

encouraged the new man to answer him brazenly, which would not do.

"*My* life ain't been no bed of roses," Harris said, voice rising halfway to sarcasm. "But *I* don't steal."

"No," Davies mused, not entirely convinced that the man standing before him had never stolen anything, "and that is a good quality to find in a policeman, the reluctance to steal. Go on with you now, Mr. Harris. Your shift is nearly over. And it is Christmas Eve. Go on with you and go in."

Harris looked up the tracks toward the yards. Smoke rose from the boilers and the offices. He glanced around at Davies a last time.

"You shouldn't stay out here all alone, Captain," he said. "After what happened over in—"

"Go on with you now," Davies told him. "And I will follow after."

There was a great deal more to say, of course. That a policeman never should allow himself to show fear, nor even speak of it among comrades. And that he himself did not fear the people among whom he had lived his life. Not even now. Their vengeance was weakened by hunger and the long years of animal loads placed on their shoulders. Their anger was more apt to be taken out upon their wives than upon a man in the uniform of authority.

Each company patch and every town was different from the next; each had its own ways about it. Davies's valley had always counted among the productive and peaceful. The men—the Irish broken to the bit well over a decade before, when those accused as Mollies were hanged without mercy, or the new arrivals, the slender Italians, noisy and dog-eyed, and the big, quiet Poles and Slovaks with their hands smashed and broken by labor of every kind—they might say in their cups that they would kill him one day. But they were far more likely to go at one another with bare fists, or to break a wife's jaw.

Davies had no fear of the miners. But he had begun to fear himself in the course of the strike. His love of order was such that he had talked himself into an old man's views before he reached thirty years. Those views had only stiffened with the decades. He did not imagine that the great men whose orders he carried out were kindly or generous. He was not a fool. But he rarely had thought them unfair to those below. A man took a job, or left it. If he took the work, he accepted the company's terms. And he owed fair labor for the wages agreed upon, whether paid by the ton or the hour.

David Davies liked a straightforward world.

And now the world had gone crooked. Despite himself, he knew too much of the calculations behind the strike, a business the workers imagined to be their own initiative, their great, shining hope. All of it had been foreseen by the colliery lords. The strike would run up the price of coal stockpiled by the big companies, while driving the smaller operators into bankruptcy. And the pits and yards could be cleansed of troublemakers. The miners would learn a lesson about unreasonable demands. Their payment for each ton they mined would go down a few cents, not up.

It all seemed a new age to Davies, and a bad one. He had earned his manhood in coalfields shaped by struggles on all sides, where nothing came easily to any man, not to the man who held the lease or to the men who worked down in the shaft. And war, brute war, made comrades of the many. The men who returned to shed their blue coats were relieved to face only the lesser risk of the mines. With butties by their sides who had proven trustworthy in battle and by the campfire.

But now the great companies were growing ever larger, until they seemed little countries unto themselves, with their own laws and men to enforce them, and the gulf between the plush sorts who rode in carriages and those whose labor paid for the matched teams that pulled them seemed to grow ever wider. For the first time in his life, Davies had begun to question those whom the Lord had placed above him in authority. There were passages in the Bible he could no longer bear to read, and hymns that nearly choked him.

He told himself that his doubts would pass with the strike, after the world returned to its proper order. He sought to remain convinced of that as the company's directors ordered the evictions of the unskilled laborers who might be easily and more cheaply replaced, then of the licensed miners who were insufficiently docile. Then, two weeks before Christmas, the order had come to keep the coal-pickers from the roadbed of the railway, every inch of which was company property.

Of course, the cars were loaded now by strikebreakers. Men whom it was his duty to protect. Men who drank too much and took too little pride in themselves. Men the company never would have hired in years gone by. Men who worked cheaply, but badly, and who did not follow the safety rules below.

And those among whom he had lived his life after leaving Wales behind at the age of fourteen, men and women with whom he had exchanged common greetings for decades, passed him by in silence now, with sullen looks or studied disregard.

The approach of this bleakest Christmas deepened the bitterness.

The company patch by the colliery and the little town above it had divided as sharply as his adopted country had divided in his youth. Davies read the side on which a man stood by his attitude in the street. He had become conditioned to men's respect, if not affection. But the miners who once would have tugged their caps pretended not to see him.

The men who stood on the company's side, those who feared disorder, the foremen and clerks, the shopkeepers and professional men, were even more effusive in their greetings than they had been before the strike. Davies was their champion against the lesser orders from whom they had drawn their lifelong living, a bulwark against men they feared might cast bricks through their windows or come to their homes bearing torches, insulting their women and worse. It was as if the fears and even hatreds had always been there, lurking, invisible, waiting to emerge.

A church bell tolled. Its metal was cheap and the flat clang suited the cold.

Happy Christmas, Captain Davies," the young policeman said, rising from the bench where he had been pulling on an India-rubber boot.

"It's early you are, Mr. Morgan," Davies said. "Happy Christmas to you. Is Harris still here, then?"

The policeman shook his head. He was as long-faced and black-whiskered as Davies himself. A fellow Welshman. As were so many of the Coal & Iron Police.

"He took himself off like a bullet, that one did. He said you told him to go on. For Christmas." Morgan's expression added, "And no loss to any of us, that one's going."

Davies nodded. "Good of you it is to take the shift for Cuffy Williams."

"No such thing, sir, no such thing. He has his wife and the lads on Christmas Eve. For me, there is no difference, see."

But there was a difference for every man, and Captain Davies knew it. Tapper Morgan was a good lad and a good policeman. He had family aplenty, if not yet a wife, with whom he would have been happy to spend the eve. But he was a true buttie and would have worked the shift twice over to send Cuffy Williams home in time for his Christmas Eve supper.

"Then I will go on myself," Davies said. "It's Reese on with you tonight, is it?"

"He's in, sir. He's just gone down to see after the mule barn."

"Well, you will pass my Christmas wishes to him. And you know where to find me, if I am wanted."

Morgan smiled. He knew where to find Davies. And everyone else in the valley. He was a confident young man, who would rise. Reese was another matter. The latter mooned about too much and now he was punishing himself by working Christmas Eve. Because his latest sweetheart had refused him in order to accept a surveyor's assistant from Tamaqua.

"Well, I am off, then," Davies said.

"Happy Christmas, Captain."

Morgan crouched to pull on his other boot.

🦅

Captain Davies climbed the street, careful in the not-quite-frozen mud. The tiny double houses, weathered gray, exuded a chill as if it had grown colder in their rooms than in the world without.

The old resentments and new hatreds had been passed down to the children. A band of them paused from scraping up snowballs in a well-yard. They glared as if he had done evil to each one of them.

Well, perhaps he had done evil. He could no longer say. He had done the duties asked of him, as decently as he could, only to find himself trapped in the middle of things. Perhaps, he thought, a man always had to choose, one side or the other, and stick to it.

Of course, he had chosen his side long before, that was the truth of it. When he first put on the company's badge and its midnight-blue uniform. Oh, he had dealt easily enough with the drunkards and petty thieves, he had quieted the feuds between families and congregations, and he always had seen to the safety of the pay chest. Even when the Mollies were at their most dreadful, with powers half true and half imagined, the miners around him had gone about their business, treating him as a fixture of their lives, not as an enemy.

On the barren hillside between the patch and the lower edge of the town, he chanced upon Michael Maloney, a miner long since pennied off after losing an eye and an arm. Grizzled and nearly toothless, Maloney lived on the broad shoulders of his sons and what whisky he could come by.

Despite the poverty of the season, Maloney had located liquor enough to make him stagger. With the muck and mire tugging at his shoes, he waved his remaining arm for balance and sang not of Christmas, but of old Ireland free.

As he recognized Davies—not ten feet away—Maloney drew himself up and made a fist.

"I swear before ye . . . Jesus Christ and all the saints in Heaven . . . I do swear . . . swear . . . ye just take that badge off, Dirty Davies . . . take it off, bucko . . . oh, I'll land ye a puck in the mouth ye'll never forget . . . and that I will . . . ye and . . . all the other black-hearted Coal & Irons . . . I'll knock yer blocks off, the lot o' ye."

"Good day, Mr. Maloney." Davies touched the visor of his cap. "Happy Christmas."

"An't he red-faced now, and not from the cold?" the drunkard asked an invisible audience. "It's shamed he is for driving off women and children . . . no more than a dirty driver, that one is . . . a driver for Pharaoh's chariots, that's what he is . . . black o' heart, black in the heart . . . as black as every Welshman what come before him. . . ."

Davies tried to step past the man, but Maloney moved—awkwardly—to block his path. Shaking his fist in the captain's face. Teetering.

"Take off that badge, ye dirty, little man . . . and I'll give ye such a puck, ye won't soon forget where it come from. . . ."

"Go home now, Mickey," Davies said. "They'll be missing you, they will."

It was an artful thing, his manner of speaking, a perfectly chosen tone that Davies had learned down the years. The right voice used against a man was better by far than a truncheon. Davies knew that many a man only wanted to have his say while the courage of liquor was in him. And no harm done to anyone who wasn't a fool entire.

The old man seemed to shrink. Bluster failing, he shambled off. Waving his one arm and singing madly of Wexford.

At the rough-cut edge of the town, a group of boys and girls, still young enough to mix, sang at the sight of him:

> *Coal an' Iron,*
> *Iron an' Coal,*
> *Bury 'im down*
> *In a deep, dark hole!*
>
> *One-sie, two-sie,*
> *Coal an' Iron cop,*

Whack 'im on the fanny
With a shaving strop . . .

Davies smiled and wished them a good holiday. But the rampart of their dislike was impenetrable.

Thereafter, he entered a kinder world, where tidy shops kept up appearances, despite the hard times, and holiday greetings had been soaped neatly upon the windows of the drummer's hotel. Mrs. Rutherford, the doctor's wife, paused in her belated holiday shopping to query the captain about a rumor of gypsies entering houses by night. He assured her that her every fear was groundless, and she stepped along with her string bag full, headed toward the commanding Episcopal Church. And Mr. Talent, who owned the hotel and commercial stable both, asked about an equally false rumor that the governor had applied for troops to be sent to Primrose and Minersville, on the other side of the county.

The holiday greetings passed in the street had a hollow sound this year.

None too soon he was safely in his refuge, the rented rooms at the back of Mrs. Evans's second floor, with the door shut behind him and the iron stove freshly lit by his landlady, its young heat fighting the entrenched cold of his sitting room, smelling faintly of sulfur. His greatcoat and dirtied boots were below in the entryway, where young Samuel Evans would clean the footwear for his daily penny, and the slippers on the captain's feet had begun to warm to his body. He took off his uniform tunic and pulled on his old brown jacket for a bit of comfort. He still had time to rest himself before getting dressed for chapel.

Yet, he did not linger by the loveliness of the coal stove. He did what he did each and every day. He went into the bedroom, where the warmth had not yet advanced. The lamp wanted lighting in the early dusk.

He lifted the shield and placed it delicately on the embroidered cloth. A lucifer match illumined the world for an instant, then the flame lowered and steadied. He turned up the wick and lit the lamp, then sat on the edge of the bed.

He saw her clearly then, as he saw her every day at the same hour. Nor was it only the photograph he saw—the image served as a silent bid to conjure the ageless woman. In the picture frame, his Bronwen looked stiff and even harsh, although she had been the softest, gentlest woman who ever lived.

It was a lie, a great lie, what they said about time healing the heart. About the easing of memories. For almost sixteen years, since his young wife coughed her life away, she had remained as present to him as if she had died that morning.

As if she had never died, had never left him.

"Oh, Bronnie," he said, "it has been a bad day, this. If I could but hear your voice, Bronnie . . . just one word . . . a word would put me right. If I could hear but a whisper from you, I'd know what to do and I'd do it."

He had learned through the years to talk to her easily, even more easily than he had been able to do during her lifetime, when he had been stiff and proud with youth and possession. When he did not hear her voice, not even the voice of memory, he spoke on, telling her of the troubles of the time and the trials of the day.

"Bronnie, do you remember Mary Murphy? Who married young O'Kane, that one? Oh, Bronnie *fach,* I had to do a terrible thing today. It shames me so. . . ."

The captain slumped as he never would have allowed himself to do in the presence of another living creature.

"It's Christmas Eve," he whispered. "It's Christmas Eve, Bronnie, and I'm lost without the sweet, forgiving touch of you. It's lost I am, and I don't know what to do. . . ."

His work had taught him early on that men were wildly different. Some could transfer love as easily as they could switch between a mug of beer and a nickel glass of whisky. But he had only had love enough to give to a single woman. Or perhaps the woman he had chosen—or who had chosen him, the truth be told—had been so rich with love herself that she had consumed a life's allotment in half a dozen years. His temples grayed, though his whiskers remained black, but he never looked twice at another woman.

Men thought him hard of heart, and women found him dour. But it was only that his heart had been given and he would not take it back. On the day his wife had died, his life had been taken, too. Twice only, he had gone down to the cribs in Pottsville. Years before. The doing of that had only made him lonelier, leaving him with a sense of shame and treachery.

He was still married. Death made no difference in that. He owed his wife fidelity, in this world and the next. The Irish

Catholics, at least, should have understood that, with all their goings-on. But all of them, Protestant and Catholic alike, only wondered at him, a man with a good income, respected by the respectable, who chose to live alone in rented rooms.

They did not understand that he wasn't alone.

"Bronnie, my love," he said a last time. Then he rose to dress for chapel.

※

They sang. The Reverend Mr. Jones was not a hard one in the pulpit. He took his lead from the Gospels, not Revelation. Perhaps, Davies often thought to himself, the pastor saw that a miner's life was punishment enough. That eve, he preached a message of love that many another Methodist would have frowned upon as insufficiently punitive to the wicked. The shepherd was deemed a poor one who neglected to chide his flock. Christmas Eve or no.

After the warmth of fellowship and rubbed shoulders in the pews, it was arranged, as it was each year, that Davies would take his Christmas Day dinner with the Griffiths family, at four o'clock exactly. Then it was off in the cold dark, four street-lamps up the hill and a turn to the left, for an hour of manly comradeship at the choral society, where the only division among Welshmen lay between those who took their punch "with spirit" and those who heeded the chapel's warnings on drink.

You would not have known the difference in the clean, little hall between that Christmas Eve and any other. Treats covered a side table, sent down from proud kitchens, food in plenty to serve for a widower's supper. The Welshmen who belonged to St. Davy's were of the sort who had risen to be pit bosses below or yard foremen aboveground, or who rendered unto Caesar in the countinghouses or shops, fellows who saved diligently and met only worry, not terror, in hard times. They were not the rich Welsh, like the Johns family of St. Clair or Colonel Jones in Pottsville, but they had gotten themselves up to solid positions that let a man care properly for his family and dress his daughters in white frocks in the summer.

They sang, for the chapel hymns had only awakened their voices. To sing was to forget the times, to disappear into the beauty of the thing. Davies himself had a prized, high baritone, capable of taking a tenor's place, should the choir need such strengthening. They sang in Welsh, and they sang in English, filling the night beyond with disciplined harmonies, wishing God's rest upon merry gentlemen or decorating the world with holly and ivy, inviting unseen listeners to strike the harp and join an earnest chorus, then finishing up, as ever, with "Men of Harlech," a song for every season in a Welshman's life.

Then that, too, was done. All the holiday greetings were passed, all the hands shaken and the good-byes said, as the members thinned away. And Captain David Davies of the Coal & Iron Police found himself alone on the planks of the sidewalk, a bit afraid of what he now intended.

Slowly, by an act of will, he turned himself up the last stretch of the hill, with the cold stinging his ears below the rim of his derby. He climbed to the street that ran just below the ridge, where a row of single homes increased in size until they reached the gates of a gabled mansion. Built to imitate the homes of the gentry back in Britain, the great house looked across the valley in fair weather and sheltered one of the heirs of the company, a Philadelphia man with a Philadelphia wife and Philadelphia children, all of whom would return to Philadelphia once young Mr. Dickinson finished his service in the field, having mastered the ways of the mines and collieries firsthand. The lordly young man was born to look out of fine windows, not to stand on the outside looking in. The summer past, his wife had been painted full-length by a fellow named Eakins, which seemed to the chapel women a marvelous sin.

The sounds of laughter and a piano well played drifted down from the brilliance of the mansion. At the gate where the drive commenced, the policeman on duty touched his gloved fingers to his cap, nodding his head to the captain.

"Good evening, Mr. Andrews," Davies said. "A happy Christmas to you, then."

"Happy Christmas, Captain. A cold one, though."

"That it is, so it is. But your bed will be all the warmer when you come to it."

Davies went up the graveled lane that wished to be elegant but could not quite escape the local roughness. Several carriages, all from the valley save one, stood beneath bare trees. The coachmen huddled together, shifting from one foot to the other and complaining. Kept in harness and ready, the horses breathed heavily under their blankets, clouding the night with steam.

The drivers tipped their hats respectfully as they recognized him. It was not a time when a man who had work wished to lose it by showing his true feelings.

Davies climbed the steps and pulled the bell chain.

A servant girl, Irish as penance, opened the door. Davies caught the quick flash of distaste that lit her eyes. The Irish were loyal against the world, though they fought among themselves in an enemy's absence.

At his request, she summoned young Mr. Dickinson. The heir's pace increased as he left his party behind and approached the front door. Startled at himself, Davies realized that he had overlooked the import of his appearance on such a night.

"Everything is fine below," he said quickly, to reassure his master, "as quiet as you could wish it." He removed his cap. "Happy Christmas, sir."

In the half-light cast by the lamps, the young man's expression shifted from concern to annoyance.

"Merry Christmas, Davies," he said, as if it was a bother to say so much. "What is it, man?"

"I . . ." Davies took a good breath. ". . . I only wanted to tell you of a thing I mean to do, sir. So that you will not think it done behind your back, Mr. Dickinson . . . so that—"

"Whatever are you talking about?"

"I want to buy the coal that is bagged for sale in the Number Two yard."

His master's face closed in, tightening until the young man looked of middle age. "Why on earth would you want to do that? What's this all about, Davies? Is this some sort of tom-foolery? I have guests, you know." Standing in the doorway, he crossed his arms and looked down at the captain. He did not ask Davies into the warmth of the hallway.

"No, Mr. Dickinson, it is not tomfoolery. I only want to buy the coal that is bagged for sale in the yard."

The younger man assumed an exasperated look. "Well, what on earth has that got to do with me? I'm not a clerk, for God's sake. Go see Smithson, if you want to buy yourself a load of coal."

"Yes, sir. I will go to Smithson, sir. But I wished you to know the reason of the thing."

"Look here, Davies. I respect your loyalty to the company and all that sort of thing. Your reputation and so forth. But I do have guests. It's Christmas Eve, you know."

"Yes, sir. But I wanted to let you know that I intend to see the coal given to the miners and their families."

There. It had been said. And Davies knew that, whatever else might come of his words, he would never see the longed-for promotion now. At best, he would end his working days walking the valley.

"Why on earth—for God's sake, man, why would you want to do a foolish thing like that?"

"Because they're cold."

The young man crossed his arms again. "Well, whose fault is that? Oh, come now, Davies. Perhaps you've gotten some sort of Christmastime notion into your head . . . I know how you feel about the new rules against gleaning from the railbeds. But you wouldn't want to go against the company's policies, would you? After all these years?"

"Is it the company's policy for them to be cold, then?"

"That . . . is impertinent."

"I withdraw the comment, Mr. Dickinson. But I want to buy the coal. As it is for sale, see."

"You've always upheld the law, Davies."

"And I will uphold it still." The captain stiffened. "If you doubt me, Mr. Dickinson . . ."

"No. No, I didn't mean that, of course. But look here. They won't be grateful to you, you know. They're likely to hurl it right back in your face."

"They will not know who gave it them."

"Even so . . . look, what good will it do? You'll spend your savings. And a week from now they'll be as cold as ever."

"But they will be warm for a week."

"And if I tell Smithson not to sell you the coal?"

"The coal is for sale. If you forbid me to buy it, Mr. Dickinson . . . I would regard that as . . . as not the doings of a gentleman."

"Are you threatening to quit your service, Davies?"

A woman's face—almost lovely, but one cut of bone too severe—appeared at the young man's shoulder.

"What's the matter, Henry? Oh, Captain Davies! Is anything—"

"Nothing's the matter, darling. Nothing at all. I'll rejoin you in a moment." The heir smiled. It was a tight, mean, unforgiving smile. "Captain Davies wants a lump of coal for his Christmas stocking. That's all."

His wife looked at him quizzically, but turned back to her guests. She did not wish the captain pleasant holidays.

"I only wanted you to know what I was doing," Davies said. "I did not wish to do the thing on the sneak, sir." But his tone was not as confident as his words. He felt himself oddly weakened now. His resolve had not lessened, but somehow something remained to be said, something to repair the other man's opinion of him. But he was not given another chance to speak.

"Do what you like," the young man told him. "It makes no difference. Now, if you'll excuse me?"

He shut the door behind himself. The piano within took up an English music-hall song.

Davies stopped by Mr. Smithson's house, paid him two hundred dollars and took a receipt with the buyer's name left blank. This time, Davies did not try to explain himself, but only extended the money. Next, he went to the livery stable and roused old Benjamin Fenstermacher, who was always a little drunk, but never too drunk to earn an extra dollar. A Dutchman and an outsider, the man could be counted on to keep his mouth shut. He bought no drinks for others, and none bought drinks for him.

They took a wagon down the hill, applying a great deal of brake against the freeze, as the Irish and Poles returned from late Christmas mass at their separate churches. After telling the two policemen on duty no more than they needed to know,

Davies had Morgan unlock the commercial yard, then sent the young man on his way. With Dutchie Fenstermacher complaining all the while, the captain and the stable hand loaded the wagon full of hundred-pound sacks.

It was filthy work, a hint of the miner's life.

❋

They emptied the wagon, quietly, by the steps of the Irish church. Then they went down for a second load, followed by a third, with the patch gone hard into hopeless, hungry sleep. Thereafter, they hauled a load to the Polish church and the last lot of the night went to the barn with the odd cross set above it where the come-lately Slavs prayed their strangeness. At last, in the bitter hours of morning dark, with the valley as still as a long-deserted mine shaft, Davies fixed the anonymous receipt to the Irish priest's front door, with a notation citing the number of additional tons that could be drawn from the yards—to be shared among the several congregations.

All through their labors, Davies had been ready to explain himself, if challenged. But Dutchie Fenstermacher didn't ask him anything, except how many more loads they had to ferry. When they finished with the night's labors, the Dutchman took his money and team and went his way back to the stables, as if it had all been as ordinary as dirt.

Before he let himself into his rooms, Davies washed himself at the pump in the yard. The handle creaked and he thought his bones did, too. The water was painfully cold.

When he went to bed, he could not face the picture of his

wife. He felt embarrassed, but could not explain why, and he slept with his back to her. He did not feel himself to be a generous man dispensing bounty. He felt neither righteous nor good and saw only deficiency in the world. With the blankets pulled high, he lay worrying that he had thrown his career away for the sake of a silly whim.

✳

On Christmas morn, the captain rose wearily, but punctually. It was the only morning of the year when the colliery whistle did not blow, but his body was so conditioned that, even reduced to a sleep of hardly two hours, he woke wide-eyed and ready.

Between his going to bed and the hint of morning, a toss of snow had powdered the valley over. Not an inch, the amount was enough to make the world seem born anew. Davies had his breakfast and gave the landlady's son a Christmas gift of twenty-five cents, then took himself down to the yards.

A normal Christmas would have seen the town and the patch full of life in the struggling light, with children yelping early in the streets and the smell of frying ham rich in the air. Instead, the captain saw only bundled figures hurrying back to outhouses.

As he strode past the shanties down in the patch, a snowball struck him just below the eye. The rock inside it hit him like a fist, tearing the flesh of his cheekbone.

He bent over, despite himself, clutching at his eye. And he heard the laughter of children fleeing into the morning shadows.

There was little enough blood, and none to speak of on the breast of his greatcoat. He had been hurt far worse in his time. It was only that he had been surprised, unprepared for the blow or the wicked hurt of it. Unreasonably, he had expected better of the world.

In hardly a minute, he straightened himself and continued on his way.

In the guardroom, he reviewed the lines left in the log by the night-men. Nothing had happened and little had been written. But the captain was glad to see that Morgan had not thought it necessary to note his activities in the book.

The two day-men were out walking their early rounds and Davies was glad of it. He sat a good while, alone by the stove, touching the cut on his cheek and watching phantoms.

When Captain Davies rose, he rose abruptly, with the light of day full in the windows, gray as age.

He spotted Harris, the new man, down along the railway line, where the policeman had been prowling for his quarry. When he recognized the captain at a distance, Harris hurried toward him. The policeman had an old man's puffing stride, long before he had earned it. Short of breath, he drew himself up before the captain, tapping the frozen earth with his foot like a horse impatient for the groom's attention.

"Happy Christmas, Mr. Harris," Captain Davies said.

But Harris had no time to spare on niceties. He was aching to pour out a tale. Then he noticed the wound on the captain's cheek.

Davies tracked the fellow's eyes and said, "A minor matter,

Mr. Harris, no great harm. Now, what is the matter? You have the look of talk upon you."

"Look at that!" the policeman cried, waving heavy arms. "Just look at that, would you?"

"At what, man? What's the matter with you?"

"Over there. Look. The houses."

"What about them?"

"The chimneys! Their chimneys are smoking! It started half an hour ago. There's more of 'em every minute. They must have been in here all night, stealing coal. They must've got into the yards."

"Perhaps they did not steal it, Mr. Harris."

The policeman dismissed the thought. "Well, how else would they get it?" He seemed to want to burst through doors and arrest men in the hundreds.

The captain let a moment pass as he stared at the ranks of houses climbing the hill. The lads had wasted no time, that much could be said for them. Once the coal was discovered, its journey had been swift to hearth and stove. Chimneys had come to life by the dozens and the calls in the distance did not sound unhappy.

It was a small enough matter. He saw that now. Even foolish, in its way. Mr. Dickinson had been right, of course. For if they would be warm this day, there would still be little enough food or little enough happiness by those firesides. More things begged to be put to rights than a few bags of coal could do.

And yet, for all his new fears over his future, Captain David Davies did not face that Christmas morning with regrets.

"If they didn't steal the coal, how did they get it?" Harris demanded. "You tell me that, Captain." It was a plaint of outraged disappointment.

Yes, Davies told himself as he considered the man who wore a badge and uniform like his own, we would have done, you and I, for Herod's henchmen, riding into Bethlehem. Going after the children. In obedience to an unjust, wicked king.

"Perhaps some poor fool meant to do them good," Davies said in his calm, usual voice. "Perhaps the coal was a gift. A Christmas gift."

The new man snorted at the absurdity of the thought. "Well, he'd have to be one damned big fool, that's for sure, whoever did a crazy thing like that. Throwing good money away on the likes of them. He'd have to be the biggest fool on earth."

"Yes," the captain agreed, with a newfound smile.

We Kings

I always liked the shepherds
Better than the kings.
I don't believe those Magi
Heard the angels sing.

The kings had an agenda
For the rumored birth.
They'd heard a king of kings would come
To rule heaven and earth.

The rumor was alarming,
Astrologers opined.
They warned of mighty powers
Conjured in Palestine.

The kings consulted oracles
Courtiers and advisors:
Discussions were unhelpful.
The wise kings were no wiser.

So Kaspar said to Melchior,
"Let us go and see
If we can make an ally
Of this King of Galilee."

"Our states are frail," Melchior agreed,
"our armies weak and small.
Better to pay tribute now
Than wait and lose it all."

And so they made their journey
With passes begged of Rome.
The roads were rare and primitive.
The three kings longed for home.

The monarchs were disgusted
When they saw Him in the hay.
Melchior told Balthazar,
"We've thrown this *trip away.*

"Gold and frankincense and myrrh,
Wasted in this squalor!
When I get that astrologer,
I'll shake him by the collar. . . ."

When husbands gray and ragged
Tell of virgin births,
A king can only shake his head,
Suppressing acid mirth.

Kings know that when God's son appears
He will shine forth in glory.
He won't be born in a cattle burn,
And that's the end of the story.

Profoundly disappointed,
Those wise kings turned and left.
They felt outraged and cheated,
Bewildered and bereft.

The shepherds, on the other hand,
Went wild with delight.
Angels danced above their flocks,
While music filled the night.

It was an entertainment
To make a poor man stare—
Better than Jerusalem
At the annual cattle fair.

They left their flocks untended,
—Which shepherds never do—
And ran downhill to Bethlehem
To kneel to the King of the Jews.

So it goes with miracles:
Kings want explanations.
Mumbo-jumbo will not do
For the politics of nations.

And you and I, are we like kings
Who cannot trust in grace?
Do we turn away as the shepherds kneel
To God with a human face?

Appearances

Christmas Eve, 1918

The colonel watched the children climb the hill, marching like little soldiers. Their wardens walked beside them, admonishing the boys as sergeants might whenever tiny legs lost step or tripped over cobblestones. Severely erect and sourly proud, the director of the orphanage led the procession, his height increased by the top hat of German officialdom. You might have thought the column on its way to an execution, rather than to a dinner on Christmas Eve.

"Ain't that just like 'em, though?" Sergeant Major Brady said, leaning over the rampart. "Ain't it just? To have 'em strutting in ranks like that when they're hardly two steps from the cradle. Have you ever seen anything like it, Colonel, sir?"

The sergeant major's breath plumed over the townscape. Everything about the man was hard. Except for his eyes. The jut of his jaw and the seen-it-all-boyo expression that masked his face could not quite hide the loneliness in those eyes. The loneliness of Christmas far from home. Nearing fifty, the regimental sergeant major was a regular with a young wife and infant son, into whose embrace he would soon retire.

"They don't understand it yet," Colonel Nichols said. "Being defeated. They're clinging to what they know. That's all."

"Well, begging your pardon, Colonel, sir," the sergeant major said, "it's time they was after learning something new. They've done marching enough, that lot."

The colonel would have liked to reply openly and warmly. But he understood the importance of keeping up appearances, even with a man he knew so well, with whom he had shared the endeavor of war at its worst. He sensed that Michael P. Brady, enlisted man though he was, would understand the words he longed to speak far better than any of the regiment's officers. But the colonel chose silence. The smoke and chill of the afternoon draped over the two men.

Colonel Lasswell Nichols did not display his emotions. That was the one luxury he could not allow himself. During the war, it had been essential for the men to imagine him as a superior being, wiser, stronger and incorruptible, to be trusted in matters, literally, of life and death. And his soldiers *did* believe in him, blind to the doubts he took such pains to hide. They followed him to the Marne, to the Meuse and beyond. Again and again, his regiment had been tasked to lead the division's attacks, through clouds of poison gas and storms of machine-gun fire.

And the colonel had *led* his regiment, refusing to lurk in a bomb-proof in the trenchlines. If he had learned anything in his career, it was the art of inspiring a soldier's confidence. He had long since abandoned the need to be liked. His profession demanded that he earn respect, not love.

The colonel had served from the prairies with their Indian ghosts, to gritty campaigns in the Philippines, from the dust of garrisons left behind by an expired frontier, to the endless miles of Sonora. He had read Xenophon by lamplight, after tracking down broken Indians who quit their reservations. He married a splendid Philadelphia girl, only to take her beyond the end of the railroads, to crumbling forts neglected by the War Department.

Yet, Isabel *insisted* on her happiness. She gave him daughters and never questioned her lighthearted choice of a husband, made in the course of a holiday dance at Bryn Mawr. He loved her dearly, with a passion she accepted in lieu of comforts. She had mastered the art of smiling through worry and sorrow, a skill he never learned. He wondered how badly her life had disappointed her.

His wife was the only one of them all who knew the extent of his pride, his vanity. She endured his divided loyalties, his devotion to his other, greater family. The only criticism Isabel ever offered had come when his uniform changed from blue to khaki. She thought blue more distinguished.

He remembered a feeble Christmas tree in Kansas, and young smiles.

Abruptly, the colonel set aside all thoughts of those he loved. But he let himself dwell on soldiering just a bit longer.

Yes, he was a proud man, good at his profession. But nothing else in his career had given him as much pride as knowing that he never had thrown away a single soldier's life, if he could prevent it. When the regiment marched from France through Luxembourg, entering Germany as part of the army of occupation, the regimental rolls had lost more men to the Spanish influenza than to German bullets or shells.

He had led his men through the hell of war. Now he only needed to see them through Christmas.

Church bells pealed in the gray-brown town below the garrison walls. Sounding the hour, not celebrating the holiday. Four o'clock. With the darkness coming down.

Winding up the antique street, the ranks of children were only minutes away now. Against his will, the colonel winced as a proctor took a switch to a little boy's calves. Driving him to keep up with those taller and stronger. Yes, they needed to learn something new. The *Boche*. The Fritzes. The Heinies, the Krauts. The Huns. But it was not his job to teach them.

That was Mr. Wilson's affair. And the colonel was glad of it.

The truth was that he had not "invited" the children to Christmas Eve dinner for their own sakes. He had given them barely a thought when the idea first occurred to him. The affair was for the benefit of his soldiers, to fill the empty hours of the holiday, although he could not tell them such a thing.

The children had only become real to him when he paid his call on the director of the state orphanage, an officious Prussian sent from Berlin to discipline the dubious sons of the Rhineland. He had never seen such strictness in a barracks, with pale men in high collars and frock coats barking at children paler still in voices only the most foolish of sergeants would have employed, confounding the authority to command with the power to humiliate. The shortages of the war's last years had left the children as lean as coyotes in a drought year. Their masters, for all their pallor, did not look quite so ill-fed.

The director had received him stiffly, speaking English as icy as it was awkward, his bearing a preposterous imitation of a cabinet minister's. To the colonel's bewilderment—then fury— the old man behind the desk refused the invitation to bring the children to the *kaserne,* the complex of fortress walls and barracks on the hill dominating the town and the Rhine beyond. In a country plagued by a shortage of every foodstuff—every child the colonel had seen looked malnourished—the director insisted that state regulations made no provision for the entertainment of his charges by occupying military forces. He held up a black-bound book to stress that the circumstance had not been approved. Order must be maintained, even now. *Ordnung muss herrschen.*

Stunned, the colonel almost made the mistake of arguing on grounds of humanity and common decency, but just had the sense to avoid treating the director as his equal in authority. Instead, he ordered his adjutant and the director's pocked assistant from the room. Then, with the heavy door shut on the pipe-tobacco-and-sweat smell of the office, he informed the director that, should *Herr Oberdirektor des Kaiserlichen Waisenheims Nummer 107* fail to appear at the barracks along with every one of the orphans healthy enough to leave his bed by four o'clock on Christmas Eve, he, Colonel Lasswell Nichols, would have the director and his family shot.

He did not wait for a reply, but rose, said "Merry Christmas," and left the office.

Now the children were nearing the barracks gate, only a few minutes past the appointed time. The colonel wondered if the slight lack of punctuality was meant as a gesture of rebellion, given the German reputation for precision in such matters.

The colonel chose to ignore the truant minutes. He doubted the delay was meant as an insult. The director didn't seem the man to display even that much courage. He was simply a puffed-up clerk, used to lording it over others with his conferred authority. When threatened with a firing squad, he had paled and nearly fainted, a scene that had been a pleasure to behold.

If taken to task, a man like that would only have his revenge upon the children. The colonel wondered if they already had suffered because of his invitation. Nor did it do to tempt fate too far. He possessed no authority to shoot anyone. The threat of execution had been as empty as the barracks had been when the regiment marched in.

Yes, empty. As empty as the world seemed since the day of the armistice. The fortress had been vacant, yet spotlessly clean on its perch overlooking the town. An invalid *Feldwebel* waited with the keys, charged to ensure the orderly transfer of the buildings and all the furnishings within them. The limping NCO produced a sheaf of papers—an inventory—for the colonel or his adjutant to sign. Nichols declined, a response the battered man seemed to think impossible.

They were curious people, the Germans. Even the French had made a filthy wreck of any barracks they had been required to turn over to the Americans. But the Germans left all things in good repair, as if they had merely gone off for a week in the country.

The colonel could have been relieved of his command, even court-martialed, over his threat to the director. He might receive a reprimand, or worse, for inviting German orphans to a Christmas Eve dinner, given the antifraternization order issued by headquarters. He had broken commissary rules, as well, by ordering his supply officer to draw extra rations from the division stores.

But the colonel did not regret one bit of it. Because it was all for his men.

Few of them were regulars, conditioned to deprivation. Throughout his career, he had served with men of slight expectations, leathery enlisted soldiers who might have been disappointed at the absence of hardship, annoyed by the lack of subjects for complaint. Even the senior NCOs were seldom married out on the plains. But the men he had commanded in this war were only citizens got up in costume, volunteers and draftees, many with wives and children back home, with fathers and mothers, and holiday traditions.

Now, with the war behind them and the mud of their last marches washed away, they had nothing to occupy their minds and hearts beyond the duties of garrison life. In war, fear had bound them, fascinated them, compelled them. They had been alive in the face of death in a way that other men would not comprehend. But on this first Christmas Eve of peace, the enemy was the ghost of a mother's kiss, the recollection of a wife's embrace or a child's innocent rapacity.

Colonel Nichols knew men. He knew that the drudgery of peace could be far harder on morale than the terrible exhilaration of war. The men believed that they had done their duty and deserved to go home. They had fought hard. And they thought it unfair to find themselves among those selected to enter Germany until the armistice became a permanent peace.

He turned from the gloaming above the river and town, from the chimney smoke rising thinly from sagging roofs. The scene was far removed from the Germany of picture books. It was the drabbest Christmas he could remember, worse than the barren prairie in December.

"Sergeant Major Brady? Go down and welcome our guests on behalf of the regiment." The colonel straightened his Sam Browne belt. "I'll be along shortly."

The NCO saluted and turned to leave the rampart. Yet, the spirit of the season had taken even him in thrall, a man whose slaughter of Moro warriors had been legendary, who had saved a failing attack on the edge of the Argonne Forest by sheer contrariness.

"If I may, Colonel, sir," the sergeant major began, "I'd like to wish you a lovely Christmas Eve, sir. Handsome of you, it is," he flicked a look toward the fortress gate, "your doing for those poor brats. On our Lord's own birthday eve."

"Carry on, Sergeant Major," the colonel said.

The NCO went down the stairs as crisply as rounds snapped into a breech from a magazine. Shoe leather clapping in rapid fire. This gesture, too, was calculated. The *Herr Oberdirektor* would expect to be met by the colonel himself. Sending the regiment's senior NCO to greet him established the man's place. Later, the colonel would be cordial. But first, he would post the rules.

In other respects, though, he had taken local customs into consideration. He knew from the many German-American soldiers he had commanded that Christmas Eve, not Christmas Day, was their most important holiday celebration. That was when the children received their treats. So that was when the orphans would have their dinner.

As for Christmas Day itself, he had used his own money to purchase two hundred cases of Rhenish wine from the local vintners—but not before suggesting to the regiment's supply officer that severe punishment would result were he even to hint to another soul where the funds had originated. It would be wine enough for every man in the regiment to enjoy a couple of glasses, but not enough to see them drunk and sorrowing.

He had seen to it that every barracks bay had a Christmas tree, and he ordered a competition among the platoons to decorate the boughs with homemade ornaments. Sergeant Major Brady would judge their efforts. The winners would be relieved of fatigue duties until the day after New Year's.

Alone now, the colonel permitted himself a smile, recalling

a judgment heard through a barracks window. "Now he's got us making up Christmas gewgaws, for cripes sake, I'm telling ya. Don't the old man let up for nothing at all? He ain't got the heart of a wooden Indian, that one. And now we got to look after his little Kraut orphans. I knew the old bugger was crazy the first time I seen him."

After inspecting his uniform's good order, the colonel marched down the steps into the parade square.

The electric lamps had come on, surrounded by haloes of damp. The light seemed to make the courtyard even colder. The orphans stood in three long ranks, almost two hundred of them, attended by a dozen men in top hats and black overcoats. The ages of the officials varied, but their facial expressions were identically reserved.

The children's overgarments were hardworn and slight. The younger boys stood bare-legged, clothed in short pants even in the winter, their meager torsos propped up on white sticks. All of the children looked frightened.

Sergeant Major Brady stood near the director. The NCO looked angry.

There were only a few enlisted men about, no more than would be required to guide the children to their meal. The colonel had ordered the rest of the soldiers to wait in the barracks refectory, a cavern of wooden beams and heroic murals. He had not wanted anything to smack of military ceremony.

The regimental staff clustered near the entrance to the headquarters, while the battalion officers, defensively proud of their warrior honors, had gathered nearer the barracks. As the colonel strode across the stones, the sergeant major called the world to attention.

It began to snow.

"As you were, gentlemen," the colonel called, in his firm parade-ground voice.

The officers relaxed again, but the orphanage staff remained rigid. As if they had been assigned to guard the kaiser's imperial chamberpot. The children shivered.

A single child looked up at the dazzle of snowflakes. A slap across the back of his head knocked his cap to the ground. The child did not dare to pick it up.

Despite the weakness of the light, the colonel saw that the overcoats and hats of the orphanage staff verged on shabbiness, too. From a distance, the men had looked finely groomed and formal. Seen closer, they reflected their country's ruin.

What must it be like, the colonel wondered, to host a conquering army? The Germans were proud people, and they had been assured until the end that their *Kaiserreich* was victorious. How much had they really believed?

As the regiment entered the Rhineland, the country folk had been somber and watchful, with their women shut indoors. When quarters were requisitioned in the towns on the route of march, the local officials tried to send even the American officers to the poorest quarters, to spare their own class. Whenever that occurred, the colonel had billeted enlisted men in the homes of the leading citizens.

As soon as the colonel approached him, the director broke into apologies.

"Colonel Nichols! I must profess regret that we have arrived past the stated time! There were difficulties, you see. The children are unfortunately weakened. And too many have grown insolent. With the Bolsheviks among us, the revolutionaries . . ."

The colonel glanced down the ranks of orphans. Although they kept their faces fixed to the front, as if on punishment parade, they watched him from the corners of their eyes. Instinctively sensing where power lay, conditioned to dread it.

He did not think they looked like revolutionaries.

When the colonel encountered men such as the director, he almost sympathized with the German soldiers who had defied their officers in the wake of the armistice, tying on red armbands and marching home to cast off the old regime. Sailors had mutinied in Kiel, Red councils had formed throughout Germany, raising flags the color of fresh-spilled blood above town halls and ministries.

But the town in his charge was quiet. Waiting to see if the Americans truly were as savage as the wartime propaganda had warned.

"It doesn't matter," the colonel said. Cutting off the director, who had begun to repeat himself. "We're . . . pleased that the children are here."

He executed a perfect right-face without thinking about it and strode toward his adjutant. The captain rushed forward to meet him.

"Get those kids inside before every one of them comes down with the flu," the colonel ordered. His voice, though harshened to the edge of anger, remained too quiet for anyone else to hear. "And don't let a single one of those vultures go with them. Get those ratcatchers into the officers' mess. *Now.*"

He returned the captain's salute and marched off to the building where his German predecessors had toasted the Hohenzollerns. The entry hall was adorned with martial paintings and the heads of wild boars. A thicket of antlers climbed one wall, surrounding a regimental coat of arms. The furniture was heavy, dark, and ugly. The colonel handed his cap and overcoat to an orderly, strode into the dining room, and positioned himself by a window. He watched as Captain Braun, the adjutant, explained in his family German what was expected.

The director protested, waving his hands at the prospect of any separation from his charges. But Braun had commanded a company on the Marne, before a whiff of gas moved him to the adjutant's position, and he wasn't about to take any nonsense from the sort of man who had driven his elders to emigrate.

The colonel almost allowed himself a smile. Only to be startled by the mess steward.

"Pardon, sir," Corporal Wilcox said.

The colonel wheeled about. Too swiftly for his own satisfaction.

"Yes? What is it?"

"Are the officers to have their fill of the brandy, too, sir? I mean . . . should we pour as much as they want?"

"Half as much as you pour for the Germans. No more. The

same goes for the wine with dinner. But give them each a full glass to start. And I don't want any of your men sampling the drink, Corporal. They'll have their chance tomorrow."

"No, sir. I mean, yes, sir. I'll handle them, sir."

"And, Corporal?"

"Sir?"

"No need to pour too much for the chaplain."

The corporal nodded. He understood, of course. The colonel had done his best to shield the man until he could be shipped home. But everyone knew what had happened. Of all men in the regiment, the chaplain had broken down the farthest in the course of the war. Appalled by God's indifference.

"That'll be all, Corporal Wilcox."

The colonel dreaded the coming hours. He had invited only the minimum number of officers necessary to avoid an outright insult to the Germans. But he did not relish forcing even a dozen of his men to endure the pretentious formality of his guests.

The Germans smelled of naptha, brine, and urine. The odor of the world changed at the border.

It was worth it all, though. To give those children a few hours' reprieve. And to give his men something to do on Christmas Eve.

In a corner of the mess, a young soldier stood beside a candlelit tree, ready with buckets of water should a branch ignite. The colonel could not remember the boy's name. There were so many names, too many. And the names of the dead had a devious way of attaching themselves to the living. The dead with the blue-green skin of the gassed, or blistered by the mustard shells, their eyes blind and tormented. They always rubbed their eyes, no matter how often you warned them. And the shell-mangled bodies, those tattered by the big rounds of machine guns or pierced by a single shot. And those who died in the sweat of the Spanish flu.

He had visited the wards himself, against orders. It was odd, really. All of his military career, he had been something of a martinet about obeying orders to the letter. Then this war, its scope or perhaps the carnage, had changed him. In any given week he had broken more regulations and evaded more orders he regarded as faulty than he had done in the three preceding decades. Commanders were strictly forbidden to visit the flu wards. But he could not bear the thought of his men—*his* men—dying alone.

He only ended the visits after his division commander stood him at attention and asked, in a fury, if he thought he was Napoleon at Jaffa. He had expected to be relieved of command, frightened by that one thing in all the war. But the general sent him back to his men, with another attack to lead.

That soldier by the tree—what was the boy's name? McCourt? Maguire?

"Private Maguire," the colonel said.

"Sir?" The boy had a ruddy, earnest face, willing to please. The kind of face war did not like to spare.

"Once the gentlemen are seated, you may relax your bearing. If you keep your knees locked like that, you're going to faint. I don't want a spectacle. Understand?"

"Yes, sir. Thank you, sir. Merry Christmas, sir." The boy was hopelessly flustered.

If you gave them clear commands, they were all right. A soldier could bear anything but confusion.

Major Burkett came in first. Never late for a meal or for a drink. He was a good man, truth be told. The best. Finest operations officer in the division. They had worked closely, intimately, on matters of life and death. There had been nights when the colonel almost confided in him. Aching for someone to whom he might pour out his heart. But it was vital to keep up appearances.

" 'Evening, sir," Burkett said. "Wonder if the snow'll amount to anything."

"Too warm," the colonel told him.

The major rubbed his hands together, sniffing the air. "Well, it's cold enough for me. I'm just glad we're not back in the trenches. Smells like pork roast," he added hopefully. "Where on earth did LeBlanc come up with fresh pork?"

"You'll have to ask him yourself."

They heard the other officers approaching, along with the orphanage staff. The colonel glanced back through the window. Darkness. Lamplight. Pale flakes struck the panes, dissolving instantly.

"Well, Merry Christmas, sir," Burkett said, stepping closer. "Bet you wish you were back home with your wife and daughters falling all over themselves to spoil you. Lovely family. You're a lucky man."

"*You* always seemed a fortunate man to me, Will. With Grace. And your boys."

"I'd be a liar if I denied it. But I've never known an Army wife to keep a better table than your Isabel."

In the slow and fly-specked years before Villa crossed the border, they had been stationed together at Fort Riley, then, briefly, at Fort Leavenworth. It had been their wives, really, who became friends, first in clapboard quarters on the prairie—scorching in summer and vividly cold in the winter—then within brick walls above the Missouri. Burkett had been a balding captain then, Nichols himself a newly made major with further promotion unlikely.

War changed things.

Had it been appropriate to confide in any man, it would have been Burkett. The colonel knew he was closer in spirit to Sergeant Major Brady, but pouring out his heart to an NCO would have compromised good order and discipline. Burkett was the correct choice. But the colonel could not bring himself to speak. Not yet. The men had to believe in his greater strength, in his indestructibility. For just a little longer.

They soon filled the room, the American officers and German officials—clerks, teachers, the director and his assistant. Every face was pink-cheeked from the cold. Yet the national complexions remained unlike. The Americans gleamed with health, despite their sojourn in the trenches. The Germans looked deprived, some of them sallow to the point of jaundice. The false rouge nature had painted on their cheeks accomplished the opposite of its purpose, making them appear ailing and repulsive.

The mess steward directed the Germans to their appointed side of the table. Before the war, Corporal Wilcox had been the headwaiter at Delmonico's. He knew how to be polite to those he despised.

No one sat. They all waited for the colonel.

He strode over to his chair and sat down, determined to avoid any ceremony.

"Sit down, gentlemen," he said. "All of you."

The Germans waited until the Americans were seated. Then they waited until the director took his chair across from the colonel. Then the assistant to the director sat down. Finally, the others dropped into their places.

The atmosphere was that of a funeral, not of a Christmas Eve dinner.

"Captain Braun," the colonel said. "Interpret for me. For those who don't understand English."

"Yes, sir."

"Gentlemen . . . I hope you won't insult me by refusing my hospitality. As the officer charged with maintaining good order among your fellow citizens, I would take it amiss if you did not permit yourselves to eat—and drink—generously."

He waited for the translation, then continued. "There is only one rule of order this evening: After my initial toast, there will be no others. Rather, we shall eat and drink as each man chooses. American style."

As Captain Braun transformed his words into German, the colonel glanced toward the mess steward.

"Corporal, charge the glasses."

"Yes, sir."

"Chaplain? Would you give us a few words, please?"

The padre, who looked as if he had not waited for dinner to start his drinking, rose slowly, but spoke clearly. The words were all right, but there was no spirit in them.

They began with *Sekt*, the Rhineland's poor cousin to French champagne. When every glass had been filled to the perfect level, the colonel stood and the others, American and German, followed his example.

"Merry Christmas, gentlemen," the colonel said.

The room, heavy with history, lightened with cries of "Merry Christmas" and "*Frohe Weihnachten.*"

And they drank.

It went awkwardly at first, but the alcohol had its effect. The stiffness of the early minutes softened with the hour. The colonel had invited officers who could manage at least a few scraps of German, and some of the Germans spoke or understood English. Rigid spines eased, shoulders lowered, and the wariness felt by both parties slowly faded. The food—far from the army's standard fare—was handsomely prepared. By the time the pork came around a second time, not a few of the Germans had drunk enough hock to help themselves unashamedly. The younger officials, men who had been too weak or flawed for service in their own military, ate like wolves.

And when the courtyard rang with the noise of children led off to view the soldiers' Christmas trees, the orphanage officials paid more attention to the passing of bottles seized from the hand of the steward.

As the last crumbs of apple pie were cleared from the table, voices erupted from the other side of the parade square.

A group of soldiers were singing. A Christmas carol.

Men in adjoining barracks took up the melody. In hardly a minute, it sounded as if an entire army had formed a chorus without the walls of the mess.

Every one of the officers present looked at the colonel. The Germans followed their eyes and stared at him, too.

Colonel Nichols stood up, but waved at the others to keep their chairs when they tried to rise along with him.

"Another round of coffee, Corporal Wilcox. And you may serve the brandy."

The Germans paid more attention to the word "coffee" than to the promise of liquor. Thanks to the allied blockade, it would have been years since any of them had tasted the real thing. Watching them lift their cups almost reverently, he found himself pitying adult Germans for the first time.

"Excuse me for a few minutes, gentlemen. I need to make my rounds."

When his adjutant moved to accompany him, the colonel signaled the captain to keep his seat.

He went out into the cold without his greatcoat. The stones of the parade square shone wet, reflecting the raw lamplight. Patches of snow struggled to survive, gathering in spots as random as death in battle. Big flakes destroyed themselves on the colonel's tunic.

In the middle of the little square, he paused. As if a greater force had laid hands upon him, holding him fast to the spot. He looked up at the sky, into the blackness shaking out the snow, and nearly wept. For one terrifying moment, a battle raged within him, as fierce in its way as the violence of war. But the long habit of self-mastery saved him.

He put one foot in front of the other, forcing himself onward. Toward the glowing windows of the barracks.

The men sang, "Oh come, all ye faithful." Yes. *Adeste Fideles.*

What could he have faith in now? What was left? The truth was he had always cherished Christmas, almost as a child does. For the precious hours of that bright celebration, he had let his discipline slacken and allowed his heart to rule. Remembering holidays past, he did not believe that a single one of his men could feel as weak as he knew himself to be. He found the moment unbearable.

But he knew the importance of keeping up appearances. He did not pretend to know God or to possess the least hint of wisdom. He had never had much time for that sort of thing. A practical man, his greatest devotion had always been to his duty.

And what had duty left him?

He paused, just once more, a few feet from the arch of the first barracks doorway, wondering if he had the strength to go on.

What was he good for? Really? What would have been his

role on that first Christmas? Carrying out the slaughter of the innocents? Was that what his life amounted to, after all?

A good soldier? The notion seemed a mockery after the trenches. After the ghastly dead sprawled on the wire.

What good was any of it? Even Christmas. Especially Christmas, deadly to the heart. Wasn't it only a myth, anyway? A journal he had read on a troopship insisted that Christmas had nothing to do with the actual date of Christ's birth, which remained unknown and unknowable. The early Christians had simply converted a pagan holiday they could not vanquish. And if all the world were to be counted and taxed, surely the Romans would have been sensible enough to conduct the business in temperate weather. It was far more likely that Jesus had been born in May or October.

If he had been born at all.

An unbearably lovely tenor voice began to sing "Silent Night." *Stille Nacht.* And the night became silent, indeed. The town slept in its lingering dread, with half its sons butchered for nothing. There would be few gifts given, or none, below the garrison walls. Families hardly had fuel enough to fire their kitchen stoves. They would sleep crowded together, greedy for the warmth of those they loved. Uncertain of the future, the people had been relieved of war only to live with rumors of revolution. With an occupying army in their streets.

In an instant, the colonel saw into their hearts.

After the first verse, other soldiers joined in, not quite agreeing in pitch or time from one building to another. The effect was all the more haunting for the raggedness. When the men sang, "sleep in heavenly peace," drawing out the notes until their voices failed, the colonel recalled those still-recent days when he had believed that peace would be a heaven.

He stepped into the barracks. Sergeant Major Brady stood waiting for him, as if he had known that the colonel must choose that door first.

The NCO did not call the men to attention. Nor did the colonel correct him. They understood each other on that point.

Except for the difference in size between the soldiers and the orphans, you might not have known the adults from the children. All of the barracks's neatness had been abandoned. Most of the inhabitants and half of their possessions had spilled toward the warmth of the iron stove. The Christmas tree attracted only the most sentimental souls, standing in a cold corner, its decorations forged from polished ration tins and chewing-tobacco pouches. A polished bayonet served as a steeple atop the tree, a usage the colonel thought dubious. But worse infractions would not have drawn a breath from him as he watched the men and boys mingle over their games, sprawled on the floor or using cots as tables. Man and child alike veered between hilarity and great earnestness.

The colonel noted a pair of soldiers teaching eager orphans to play poker.

"Ain't it a thing of wonder and amazement?" the sergeant major said. "They're like great, clumsy babies, the lot of them. I'll tell you the truth, sir, I wasn't sure how it would go, all this. But I haven't seen the lads this way in all my days with the regiment. When they all come back from putting away their chow—with the poor little boyos starting off afraid to eat, then mad to stuff it in—when they all come back here you would have thought you had a regiment of Red Cross nurses on your hands, for all the gentleness of 'em. Hoisting the little devils up on their shoulders, and some as weren't so little. Lugging the lot of them about like they're shunting trench mortars at the double-quick, and all of them just laughing like the bejesus." The NCO shook his head. "If those kiddos are having half the time the lads are, you've done a grand, good thing, you have, Colonel, sir."

"Nothing of the kind, Sergeant Major. Just common sense. Showing the local population that we're not going to scalp anybody. I think I'll look in on the other companies now."

"Shall I accompany you, sir?"

"Thank you, Sergeant Major. I'd rather do it alone. And you might want to have a word with Shea and Wilhelm before they start teaching those children how to palm aces."

"Yes, sir. I'll do that, Colonel, sir."

As he marched out, in a lull between carols, as soldiers caught their breath and argued over what hymn might suit them next, he heard a high, thrilling sound. In moments, it swelled louder, growing artful.

It was the sound of children singing. "*O Tannenbaum.*" Whatever the many failings of the orphanage, it sounded as though they had a polished choir.

He could not bear it then. He turned as sharply as if leading a parade and made for the rampart that looked out over the town. He even failed to return the salute of the sentries.

Alone on the high wall, he stared down through the tumult of snowflakes, toward the lamplit windows of the town. One after another, they darkened as he watched. Even the streetlights seemed poverty-stricken, their light emaciated.

He took off his hat and buried his face in it, hiding from the world. And he wept.

But not for long. He could not let his eyes go red, could not betray himself, his trust. The men could not be allowed to suspect anything.

The snow licked at his ears.

As soon as he could, the colonel forced himself to turn about, settling his cap precisely on his head. And he went through the barracks, one after another, inspecting the curious progress of the evening.

Soldiers from German families, whose fathers owned farms or beer gardens or haberdashery shops, told stories of America, of *Weihnachten* passed in Iowa or Missouri, in Pennsylvania or in New York City, tales of transformation, of love and abundance. Language skills were at a premium, more valuable in these few hours than cigarettes had been in the front line. Soldiers who had teased their comrades as "dumb Dutch" or "Kaiser Willies" now competed for the attention of those who could translate to the orphans.

Clasp knives and good luck charms emerged from pockets and packs, impulsive gifts of the heart, and the frailest orphans had pride of place at the stoves. A private whose front teeth had been lost to a German rifle butt showed enamored chidren how to whittle. Improvised checkerboards and a few compact chess sets, preserved through slaughter, commanded a level of attention most of these men would have reserved for a boxing match.

In the second to last bay, a flustered young sergeant approached him, almost as if coming to an altar rail with sins on his conscience.

"Sir," he began, with a hint of a stammer, "do . . . do you think . . . I mean . . . permission to speak to the colonel, sir?"

"Permission granted, Sergeant Campbell." He hoped he had recalled the correct name.

"Sir . . . the boys . . . I mean to say . . . couldn't we . . . I mean it just doesn't seem right, to treat these kids all right this once, then just throw 'em back in the pond. Maybe . . . couldn't we . . . couldn't the regiment sort of adopt the orphanage?"

"I'll consider your suggestion, Sergeant Campbell."

"That's swell of you, sir. That's just swell."

"I only said I'd consider it. So don't start any rumors. Understand?"

"Yes, sir. You can count on me, sir."

But the colonel knew he could not count on the sergeant. Not in this. But it hardly mattered. He'd been thinking along the same lines himself. Wondering if it might not be just the sort of project the men needed to occupy them when they had an idle hour. Sponsoring an orphanage wouldn't be the worst thing they could do. And there was another one, for little girls, in the next town. That sister institution's difficulties had been raised over dinner, by a young German teacher at whom his superiors frowned.

As he left the last barracks, the colonel found a soldier standing at the edge of a patch of snow, leaning his face to the barracks wall and sobbing so hard it resounded.

To his chagrin, the colonel could not recognize the boy from behind. Against his own sense of decorum, he laid a hand on one of the lad's heaving shoulders. And found he had mistaken his man. It wasn't a young soldier, but an NCO in his thirties, a corporal known for his fondness for the bayonet.

The sight of the colonel shocked him. Yet, the corporal was so distraught that he could not gather himself, not even in front of his regimental commander.

"I'm sorry, sir. I'm sorry . . ." was all he managed.

The snow thinned and wandered.

"It's all right, Corporal Clarke. We're still stirred up from the war. Every one of us."

The corporal shook his head. "Do you know . . ." he began, ". . . do you know, sir, that half of those kids are war orphans? Their mothers couldn't feed them. Or they died of the 'fluenza." The man's eyes burned as he stared into the colonel's face, seeking something for which there was no name. "I'm sitting there with this grinning little bastard on my knee . . . and Henninger asks him in Dutch if he knows anything about his folks. And the kid starts yapping about how his old man was killed at Verdun, 'for the Fatherland,' like he's reciting something he's had to learn by heart. I mean, Jesus, sir, I know we didn't come anywhere close to Verdun. But I started in to thinking how *I* might've killed his pop and been telling stories about what a hero I was for doing it." The corporal's eyes searched as deeply as human eyes could go. "What was the sense of any of it, that's what I want to know? All of us killing each other like that. For what, Christ almighty?"

"You did your duty. The boy's father did his."

"But what *for*?" It was a man's question, asked in a child's tone.

There were countless answers, of course. But the colonel could not bring himself to recite any of them. Because he was no longer certain he believed in them himself.

"It's over now," he said. "That's what matters, Corporal. There'll never be another war like this. I promise you that much. We'd have to be insane to go through this again."

And then he left the soldier to his sorrow. But ghosts pursued him as he crossed the courtyard.

The colonel strode back into the officers' mess, greeted by jovial voices and the pungent smell of liquor. With its fine tile stove, the room was almost too warm.

Empty bottles littered the table. At the sight of the colonel, a middle-aged German, florid now, rose to propose a toast before remembering himself.

The padre sat at the table's end, sodden with drink and quiet, his face the twin of the painting of Job in Isabel's childhood home.

The colonel singled out the regimental supply officer and led him down a hall into the billiard room. Beneath a painting of the surrender at Sedan, the colonel demanded, "Are you sober enough to carry out basic instructions?"

"Yes, sir. Absolutely, sir."

"Then pay attention. I'm not going to let those children walk back to the orphanage and freeze themselves. I want you to get on the field telephone and order up enough trucks to take the kids home. Tell them I want all Fords—they're better when it's slippery. And make sure they have their canvas up."

"Now, sir?"

The colonel reached for a front pocket, an old habit, then remembered himself and read the wristwatch he had adopted for service in the trenches. He had gone through four of them since the regiment's first entry into the lines.

"Yes, now. It'll take some time to round up the drivers and enough mechanics to get those wrecks down the hill and back. Plan to load outside the gate in one hour."

"Yes, sir."

"And one more thing. See if we can spare a few extra blankets."

"How many, sir? You know the trains haven't all caught up with—"

"Two hundred should do."

The quartermaster looked as if he had seen a bear with wings gliding around the room. "Sir . . . that . . . that's government property, if I may just—"

"You may not. Two hundred. If we have that many on hand. If not, give them all we have to spare, then requisition the remainder from division stores the morning after Christmas. What's the matter with you, Major? Haven't you understood one word I've said?"

The quartermaster had understood.

The colonel returned to his duty, enduring the inebriation of Prussian bureaucrats whose kind had ruled the Rhineland for a century, administering the inhabitants into submission, all in the name of a glorious German destiny. Now their day was over, and they knew it.

The Prussians were beer drinkers, of course. Wine crept up on them. Had the *Waisenheim* staff been forced to walk, the orphans would have had to carry at least half of them.

Herr Oberdirektor sat dully in his chair, wearing an expression so forlorn it was comical.

The chaplain's eyes had closed.

The junior officers had grown restless, as if they couldn't wait to press on to some fraternity party or hideaway saloon. Of a sudden, they all looked impossibly young to the colonel. As if this were some sort of masquerade ball to which they had been forced to come by their parents, as if they really belonged at college football matches, wearing sweaters and knickerbockers to flirt with girls as fresh as autumn air. Except for Burkett, who lingered over a last brandy, not one of the officers looked as if he had just survived the greatest war in history.

When he could no longer put it off, the colonel dispatched his adjutant to find Sergeant Major Brady. It would fall to him to put an end to the evening, to take the children away from the lonely men to whom they had been a gift.

All too soon, the colonel stood in the parade ground, wearing his greatcoat again. The snow had given up, incapable of covering the world. The air was biting and raw. Unsteady, the German officials pulled their overcoats tight at the neck, mur-

muring more to themselves than to one another. The colonel yearned to keep them away from the children as long as possible. But their charges emerged at last, chastened by the evening's sudden conclusion, no longer inspired to sing.

The little boys were led by towering men who held their hands or lofted them on their shoulders. And the colonel understood that many a lion of the battlefield would cry himself to sleep, muffling his sobs beneath his blanket, fearful that only he among them all could not master his emotions. Fearful of the judgment of men who had grown to love one another without understanding it.

Church bells rang as the trucks pulled off, a coincidence. Soldiers waved. There was no formal discipline now, no ranks or barked commands. Surreptitiously, men touched at their eyes. The children did not call out farewells. The ball was over. Returned to the tutelage of their masters, they looked back silently as the vehicles clattered down the hill, their faces small white smears in the truck-bed shadows.

And then they were gone.

As the mass of men began to disperse toward their separate barracks, one voice, a mighty tenor—doubtless Welsh or Irish, the colonel told himself—sang out, echoing strong and clear against the walls of brick and masonry.

"For he's a jolly good fellow, for he's a jolly good fellow . . ."

In a blink, a thousand voices were singing, united before the colonel realized they were singing about him. And then he was astonished.

"Which nobody can deny, which nobody can deny . . ."

He was incapable of behaving with the appropriate amount of authority for the first several verses. As soon as he could, he waved the sergeant major to his side.

The sergeant major had been singing, too. The Irish blood, of course.

"Sergeant Major," the colonel called against the racket, "that's enough now. They'll wake the town and we'll have God knows what kind of an uproar on our hands. That's enough now. The men will return to their barracks."

The sergeant major bellowed to wake the dead, in a clarion voice that might have summoned shepherds from the farthest fields—and they would have put in a prompt appearance, too.

The colonel strode off toward his own quarters, toward the room that had belonged to a series of other colonels before him, all the *Herr Obersts* who had enjoyed the big mahogany bed and the warmth of the blue-and-white-tiled stove that dwarfed even the armoire. He did not say good night or wish any man a holiday greeting.

Now, of all times, they must not think him weak.

He locked himself in his room and wept, falling asleep still half in his uniform, then waking to weep again. Crying bitterly for his wife and daughters dead of influenza an ocean away, dead in all the safety of an Ardmore mansion, dead of a plague that had spared his wife's aged parents, while glutting itself on the young.

He fell into a merciful sleep at last, with a hand laid over the faded letter he could no longer bear to reread, the letter he had received one hour after the armistice went into effect.

But the colonel woke early on Christmas morning, as he did every other day, and he yanked the bellpull beside the bed to let the orderly know he wanted his shaving water.

When he marched downstairs to make his customary rounds before breakfast, Sergeant Major Brady stood waiting for him. As always.

"Merry Christmas, Colonel, sir," the NCO said.

"Merry Christmas, Sergeant Major. Anything on the morning report?"

"No, sir. All quiet. Not so much as a fistfight."

Together, they stepped out into the first light. The remnants of snow had turned to ice on the parade square. Only a few faint trails of smoke rose above the town. Fuel was scarce and had to be preserved. But the smell of burned brown coal haunted the air. It never disappeared entirely.

They began their rounds at the front gate, where the regiment's sentries presented themselves to the town.

They were cold lads counting the quarter hours until their relief.

"Private Giacometti," the colonel said, in a stern, low, lethal voice. "Your boots look as if you found them in an ash heap. And we're not in the trenches any longer. I expect each man to shave himself properly."

Turning from the startled soldier, who clearly had expected gentler handling, the colonel told the sergeant major, "If Private Giacometti doesn't care to polish his footgear before he appears for guard duty, perhaps you could find something more ambitious for him to polish, Sergeant Major. And for his corporal to polish with him. The sergeant of the guard can lend a hand, for that matter."

The colonel strode off. He heard the sergeant major hurrying to overtake him and he knew that, on this one morning, the NCO would attempt to pacify him, to argue that it was Christmas, after all.

Just when he sensed that the sergeant major was about to speak, the colonel turned and robbed the NCO of the first—and last—word.

"Christmas or not," the colonel said, "we must all keep up appearances."

Special holiday thanks to Jack Mountcastle, Joe Webb, and Robert Bouilly, who delivered gifts of historical detail

Herod

Herod understood the business of kings:
You crush the competition,
Whether that means the prince next door,
Or a primitive superstition.

You cannot let the people hope,
You need to make it hurt:
A beggar cannot shout complaints
With his face shoved in the dirt.

So when those vagrant diplomats
Inquired about a child,
Herod played along with the game.
He gave them dinner and smiled.

And when those shabby "kings" left town,
He cut a thousand children down.

How Jimmy Mulvaney
Astonished the World for Christmas

Christmas Eve, 1928

If you don't mind, I would like to tell you about the best Christmas I ever had.

"Jimmy, you bum. Get out," Annie said, to my consternation. "I was saving that money up for the rent. You bum you. I don't know where my brains was at when I got mixed up with you in the first place, I could shoot myself for being so stupid."

"Annie," says I, "I never took that money out of your drawer, I swear to God, I wouldn't so much as open a drawer where a lady keeps her items of such a personal nature, I didn't take a penny, not one cent." Which was not quite true, but you understand a man has his needs which cannot always be explained to a woman when important business is at hand and opportunity will not wait.

"You're a liar and a no-good bum," she told me, which was not too bad, allowing for the hysterical constitution of the female species. "Get out of here before I call the cops."

"Annie, honeybunch . . ."

"You get out. Or I'll call my brothers."

Now, I did not believe that Annie would call the police, which would be unladylike, which she is mostly not. But her brothers were another story, and the story was not a pretty one. She was one of the Shenandoah Pulaskis, who were mean Polacks every one of them, except for Annie the most of the time. Her brothers were not gentlemen, as they say.

"Annie, dearest darling of mine, it's Christmas Eve. . . ."

I will admit to you that I employed what is called a tone of supplication, for the money which I did not exactly take, at least not the way she meant it, was gone and a man should never bet on the fights right before Christmas. I see that now, but hindsight, as they say, is 20/20, which is not good odds.

Annie just put on that look of hers which is enough like the look of her brothers to make a man uncomfortable with the situation in which he has found himself and she started toward the door. Which meant she would go downstairs to the phone on the wall and ask the operator for a connection to Shenandoah, which would not be helpful to me, under the present circumstances, for my boat of speculation had sailed with fond hopes but my ship had not come in. I suspected her brothers would not be reasonable. Anyway the Polacks do not like the Irish, why I do not know, and they were mad at Annie, which was a grievance they would hold against me, since they could not beat up their sister, at least not in Pottsville, where they had no connections with either the cops or even a hose company.

I decided that, as the man of the house, or at least as the

man of Annie's apartment, which she kept very nice, her Polish background considered, it behooved me to, as they say, leave the premises for a precarious length of time so that she might contemplate the folly of her ways and we might enjoy the prospect of a reconciliation, sooner I hoped than later.

"I'm going, I'm going," says I. "But you'll be sorry. I got big things in the works, don't you think I don't. You're going to get the surprise of your life, Miss Annie Pulaski, and then you'll be sorry."

"Just get out, you thieving mooch," she said, in a tone that I found wanting of the Christmas spirit, but that is how women are.

❧

Now you will call me a sentimental Irishman, but I believe that a man should always spend Christmas in the bosom of his family. And since my family and I were not presently on the best of terms and, anyway, they were ensconsed in the family manse in Scranton, to which I did not in my present circumstances of misfortune have the carfare even had I wished to suffer their unjust recriminations upon my return, Annie was the family on which I had expected to bestow my happiest affections of the season. I even had consigned myself to accompany my object of the heart to midnight mass to put her soul at rest and because, after all, it was Christmas and going to mass usually provokes Annie to a mood of Christian generosity, except when she goes to confession, which is another story.

Thus it had come to pass, as they say, through very little

fault of my own, though some was involved I will admit as an honest man, that I found myself wandering the streets of Pottsville in the dark and early hours of Christmas Eve, as bereft of lodging as the Holy Family themselves, which was an embarrassing and uncomfortable situation for a man of my social position. I must explain to you that my irregular employment at that current moment was a matter of common sense and dignity, for a man should not do work that is beneath him and I lived in expectations. I even had desisted from playing the ponies, except when money came my way with which I might do so.

I give you that my situation on that particular Christmas Eve composed an unexpected reverse, but it was not yet my Waterloo, as they say, and life's little setbacks reveal our true character. I had, if we are speaking of my general future, cause for the pleasantest hopes. The good people of Pottsville, which is a fair metropolis when you do not expect too much of a place, did not yet harbor the great prejudices against me which emanated from certain elements of question in Scranton, where I was blamed unfairly for a number of things that are not worth your attention, all beginning some years before with my terms of exit from our patriotic military service after the armistice in France, which was all a misunderstanding, since it was not my fault I was not sent to the front but was put to work laying duckboards in the port of Brest, France, and there was such an abundance of goods going to waste on the docks and in those warehouses that I thought it only right to share some of those perishable items with the poor French people with whom I did a small amount of business until I was unjustly accused by an officer who played polo, which is never a good sign.

I had made a new start in Pottsville, to which said environs I had been forced by the viccissitudes of fate, and needed only the love of a good and understanding woman to help me through a difficult stretch, when Annie showed me the door on Christmas Eve, though she calls herself a good Catholic.

Do not think for a moment that I lacked friends, though I had not enjoyed the advantage of a long residency of the sort that annoys the police sooner or later, but when you are not at your peak of employment, sometimes the friends and acquaintances with whom you are driven to consort are not all complete gentlemen, though a good heart must count for something. I did not think I would lack for a bed, but I am fastidious as a gentleman should be and believe in going to the barber every morning but Sunday, until a fellow's credit runs out, and I always tip the manicurist wherever I go because even if she is not a looker, her sister might be. That is how I met Annie. I am glad I had on a new set of cuffs that day because that is the first thing a manicurist notices, of course, except for a gentleman's rings, which were at that time absent from my fingers, due to besetting needs that had removed them. Anyway, I do not like to repose on sheets that have not been changed from the occupants previous, since I have had enough of that and more in my periods of misfortune, which I hope Mr. Hoover will change. Although he is a Republican, I always hated tearing down his campaign posters, no matter how much we were paid to do so, and not only because such work ruins a good manicure. I believe it is advantageous for our economic circumstances that he will be our new president and, though a man should always vote for his own kind, as many times as ward conditions permit, that is not the same thing as hoping his own kind will win, which is another story.

The sad truth is that my friends of the moment were not in the money, no more than was I, despite the wealth of our aspirations and valuable skills. I feared my Christmas would suffer, which is enough to bring a tear to a fellow's eye.

I was resigned to a miserable fate, although I thought I might try Annie again in a couple of hours, and it was much to my regret that the Christmas present which I had generously considered buying for her had not come into my material possession, due to said lack of funds. A gentleman must always be generous, especially at Christmas and on all such similar occasions, but Bob the Bull McGinley should have won that fight, which I think was fixed, but no one told me in time. Thus, to my great shame, I did not have a Christmas gift for the object of my affections, though she had unfairly for the most part berated me with my misfortunes, and I went up the hill past the courthouse in the direction of where Mickey O'Hara lived with his wife, I think, and their brats, hoping for dinner and mayhaps a berth for my passage to the far shore of Christmas. The truth is, as you will have perceived, that I was feeling down and out, and just at the end of my luck.

Then what should appear to my wondering eyes, as they say, but flames expelling themselves from the upper story of a house, a clapboard half-a-double matchbox one step above skid row, and out runs a woman in a bathrobe into the slush and the slop with her bare feet and starts screaming, "My baby! My baby! My baby's in the fire," which she should have thought of before she ran out herself.

I faced a dilemma. The unfortunate truth is that, at that particular time, I owned no more than one good suit, which was not only becoming worn beyond the degree appropriate to a gentleman of my social standing but which also happened to be upon my back at that very moment. I pondered whether it was worth risking the final ruination of my best duds for the sake of a baby, who, given the neighborhood, I did not expect was exactly the Christ Child, since there were Negroes living up the block, as I knew all too well from a prior misunderstanding, but the woman saw me and screamed to beat the band. I could not risk the damage to my reputation had I turned blithely away, no more than you could.

So in I went, with the woman crying out behind me, "My baby . . . he's upstairs, he's upstairs . . . my baby," and the hall was already smoky and I was no sooner inside than I'm coughing like one of those veterans who never got all the mustard gas out of their lungs, you see them on the street. It was clear as day that the shack was divided into two apartments, over and under, though it was not as genteel in nature as the edifice in which Annie has three very nice rooms. Up the stairs I trotted and into the apartment on the second floor, which was going up in a blaze-o like the Fourth of July. The woman must have been nuts, that is all I can say. In her crummy little front room she had lit candles on a Christmas tree the way the old-

timers used to do and what did she expect? Well, the baby
wasn't helping any, because it wasn't even crying so I could
find it. The truth is, as I have always suspected, that babies are
stupid and it's a wonder any of them survive, but then I found
it in a crib that wasn't on fire yet, which was a good thing for
the baby.

And out we exited, the two of us, with said infant cooing
like it's just been to the races with a winning ticket and me
choking half to death and my one good suit already singed and
smoked through like a plate of bacon.

"The downstairs!" the woman cried for all the world to
hear. And the world was beginning to gather around, though I
didn't hear any fire whistles yet and probably, being Christmas
Eve, all the boys down the hosie were drunk, anyway, but the
woman yells right in my face like I can't hear, just bellowing at
me like a cow, "Downstairs, some guy lives downstairs, maybe
he's sleeping, he'll die, he's gonna die of fixation," and all I can
think is, Lady, if he can sleep through this racket you got going,
he's dead already, but everybody was watching me then and a
gentleman has to put up a good front, so back in I went.

I kicked open the door of the bottom apartment, which not
only ruined the shine on my shoes but scuffed them like the
shoeshine boy had used sandpaper by mistake, which made me
resort to masculine language, despite the smoke, which would
have killed a man who didn't watch his health. Not to mention
my manicure, which was ruined in its entirety, and I was not
certain Annie would give me another one soon enough to main-

tain my good appearance, since some women nurse grudges up to a week.

There I was, in a burning house, on Christmas Eve, with every reason to be forlorn or worse.

I did not know it yet but that was when my fortune began to turn. The apartment, which you could tell belonged to a bachelor and lacked the woman's touch, as they say, was filthy as a French latrine, of which I have seen a few. But said apartment was not yet on fire. The electric lights still worked even, which was to prove to my benefit, but there was plenty of smoke wandering through those less than fragrant rooms and the flames above were blackening the ceiling. Fortunately, the blinds were shut and I realized that it would have been a sin and a shame to just let any valuables burn up. Waste not, want not is, perhaps, the most important rule by which a man should live, or one of the top three.

I went through the drawers, starting in the bedroom, and that was as far as I got because, though I could not believe it, under a stack of shirts in a dresser and not even locked up I found a box of bullets for a revolver, a diamond ring that wasn't bad but wasn't anything special, either, though it looked like maybe a carat, a matter I had learned to judge during one of my less successful periods in life, but that wasn't the important thing, which was the necklace. I saw before me, in the smoke, a necklace that might have been worn by the Queen of Sheba herself, if not Pola Negri, who is my favorite star of all because of the way she looks and she has class, which some foreigners do.

Now, I do not pretend to enjoy the expert nature of a pawnbroker or even a jeweler, but I can tell a real rock from glass or paste, and this necklace had more emeralds than Ireland has shamrocks in it, all laced through with diamonds themselves, emeralds and diamonds, and not set in tin, either. I mean, I couldn't count all the sparklers and didn't, but rescued said item for posterity, by putting it in my pocket along with the ring.

I should mention that there was nobody in that apartment for me to rescue, which, as a gentleman, I would have done.

Now the truth is I am excitable by nature, though I believe a mild disposition most becomes a fellow, as they say. And the smoke was getting thick and the temperature was getting as hot as the place where that polo-playing captain is going to end up eventually for his largely unfounded accusations against me in Brest, France. So I neglected to pursue my rescue of valuable items to a further extent and left the premises.

Gagging and, to tell the truth, putting it on a bit, since there was quite an audience assembled and I did not want to disappoint them, I stumbled back out into the street, where the woman with the baby from which she had fled, to my ultimate good fortune, was hollering in a now-pleasing manner, "He saved my baby! He saved my baby!" and I noted that it was a peculiarity of her speech, which was not educated, that she repeated everything twice, which would have been all right if she had been a looker, since a debt of gratitude might have been owed me and there is nothing quite like a grateful woman, but she has to be a looker, which this one was not.

The crowd, which was growing by the second, cheered me and clapped as if I had just knocked Dempsey through the ropes and won the Derby besides, which was a new and encouraging sensation to me. I had the sense to bend over and continue choking and gagging for a while longer, to allow my fellow citizens to enjoy the drama before them and I hoped I was not too disheveled, as they say, since you never know who might be watching.

The cops came and the fire wagon, and the woman with the baby was becoming altogether too friendly for my predilections, because the truth is I had Annie on my mind even when I rescued that ring and necklace. Not only was the woman with the baby lacking in specific female attractions of an appealing nature, but my Annie, though she is a Polack and there's nothing she can do about that, is a terrific gal, when she is not angry at me, and the truth is I had never had better, though a gentleman should not admit it if he is smart. I wished she was right there to see me, with the crowd cheering and the cops, for once, not looking at me like I had been shoplifting in the five and-dime, which I have never done.

Now, those of you who do not believe in the spirit of Christmas, I will tell you that you don't know a thing you're talking about, because not only had I rescued that baby and, more importantly, the necklace and the ring, but I remembered those bullets, which I had not taken because I do not believe in violence as a principle, unless it is unavoidable. As an experienced man of the world, it quickly became of interest to me that, Point A, as they say, nobody who lived in a couple of rooms in a shanty like that up behind the courthouse had gotten hold of that necklace on the up-and-up or even the ring, though they did not go together in quality and clearly came from two separate jobs. Point B, the character who had not gotten them on the up-and-up had a gun, because that is where bullets go into, and the gun was not there, but extra bullets were, so the fellow was out somewhere in the wide world, but probably not far away, maybe even in that crowd watching me. Finally, Point C, I saw with the wisdom of many a hard-learned lesson that I had no way to get rid of that necklace in a manner accommodating to its value without undue risk to my personal freedom and welfare, should questions arise from the legal establishment as to said object's origins, or maybe the guy who stole it in the first place would find out and would fail to appreciate my position in the matter or was even connected to the mob, which is something a gentleman must always take into consideration.

"Officer," says I to my fellow Irishman who was taking down my name and not the least suspicious, "if you don't mind, can we go to the station house?" Which was just down the hill from the courthouse, on Centre Street. "There's more to all this than meets the eye."

"What're you going on about?" he asked me, for the police can never do a single thing to save their lives without asking more questions than a fellow wants to hear.

So I inched closer, almost whispering in his ear. And I says, "I believe we are at the scene of a crime, so to speak."

"Arson?" he said, stepping back.

At which I rolled my eyes. "No, I don't mean arson, the fire started because that dumb cooze over there lit candles on a Christmas tree right under the roof of that crackerbox, which I can tell you because I saw what was left, but there's something else I meant."

To hint at the delicate nature of my situation, I nodded toward the crowd, which was delighted at the spectacle, with the firemen destroying what was left of the house and knocking in the next-door windows with mistaken blasts from their hoses, although I think they really were drunk and having some fun, which is what the yonkos do in Scranton, depending on which hose company comes to the rescue. The innocent bystanders, as they say, clapped and cheered as the roof fell in and a dazzle of sparks exploded into the sky. It felt as if the Christmas spirit had descended on Pottsville at last.

"Well, Mr. Mulvaney," the copper with the stripes on his sleeves said to me, in the respectful tones a policeman should use to a gentleman, "given as you've pulled that child from the fire for Gracie Thomas, who's been known to take a drink or two in her time, your credit's good with me, come down to the station, then." And the sergeant gave orders for this and that to the other two cops who had come around when it was too late to do any good, which is typical, and we start walking back down the hill, with me thinking first of all of Annie, who I must admit I was even a little bit in love with, though I was not about to tell her such a thing in the mood she was in the last time I saw her, and of how I might not be able to hold onto that necklace, but, surely, if it was hot there would be a reward, wouldn't there?

"So what's on your mind, Mr. Mulvaney?" he asked, impatient the way cops are when they're not sitting at a lunch counter, especially the Coney Island, which has the best dogs in town and pretty good coffee, though the waitresses watch you like a hawk.

"Sergeant," says I, "we have got to wait until we get to where it's safe." I looked around me. Nobody was following us that I could see. "Do you know who lived in the bottom apartment, under the woman you have spoke of?"

He shook his head. "New fellow. Sure, I've seen him around, but as long as he's been minding his own business, I tell the boys to mind theirs. No need stirring up trouble, now is there?"

Which was a sentiment with which I agreed wholeheartedly. The truth is that I had begun to regret taking that necklace out of the drawer at all, since I now could apply my imagination to see how it might bring trouble down upon my head, which would be as undeserved as it was unwelcome, but you cannot change what you have done already, truer words were never spoken.

In the station house, which smelled of the aftereffects of cabbage for dinner, if you know what I mean, Sergeant Scanlon took me back to where the cops were loafing who should have been working and, once I had all their attention, I pulled the necklace, but not the ring, out of my pocket and held it up.

"Cripes, awmighty," one of them said, who had a belly the size of which inspired confidence in him as a policeman.

"Where did you—" Sergeant Scanlon began to ask.

"I was concerned," says I, "that some individual might have been slumbering in the downstairs apartment, which nobody was, but I went in and this is what I found, it was laying right on top of the dresser. For all the world to see."

"Cripes, awmighty," the full-figured and manly copper repeated.

And that is how I knew that the Christmas spirit had smiled upon me, because a detective came out of a side office like a shot, just like he was shot from a cannon, and he bellowed until they could hear him in England and France.

"That's it! That's the necklace was stole from Old Man Reardon's place the other night. That's it, by God, that's it!"

Which was all news to me, but I should read the papers more often. I like the funnies, especially the Katzenjammer Kids, but a man in my line of work has enough to do keeping up with the racing sheets.

Sergeant Scanlon, who already had put on a mug like he had just solved the whole case himself, barked at the other cops sitting there, "Go up there right now, the pack of yous, and find out who was living in that bottom apartment. Under Gracie Thomas, up Second Street there. And bring him in, whoever he is and wherever he is."

The detective, who was old enough to be seasoned in the ways of the world, looked at me with a respect which I have not always experienced in the company of the police and said, "Young man, you've just solved the biggest crime in Pottsville this year. And very courageously, it appears."

"It wasn't anything at all, only a trifle," says I. "My name is

James X-for-Xavier Mulvaney, if the newspapers want to know."

"Well, I'm sure they will. What a great—" He stopped for a split second, just as long as a win-by-a-nose takes to cross the finish at the track, then he resumed, as they say, his discourse. "This is going to make Mr. Reardon one very happy man. And Mrs. Reardon. You just wait right where you are, Mr. Mulvaney. I'm sure he'll want to thank you himself."

By which I expected the detective meant Mr. Reardon, of whose name I had heard, for I follow matters of high finance and society, which is important at times for my line of work, would want to talk to me over the telephone, which in my folly at the time I would have preferred, for nobody had said anything about the ring which was still in my pocket and I knew that anybody who could buy that necklace would have rings to choke Diamond Jim Brady and wouldn't bother with less. Thus, I wished to leave the premises of the police station while the small matter of the ring was still in my pocket and, as you can see, virtue is its own reward.

But the detective came back and said, "Mr. Reardon's coming down to the station this minute. Leaving quite a holiday party, by the sound of it. He wants to thank you himself, in person. And to pick up the necklace, of course."

"But," says I, "won't the necklace have to be held as evidence for the proceedings of the court against the criminal who has taken it and left it laying out on the dresser for all to see?"

The detective shrugged. "Oh, I suspect the court will do just fine on Mr. Reardon's word. No need to spoil Mrs. Reardon's Christmas. Justice will be served, Mr. Mulvaney, that I promise you, although I appreciate your concern." He stood off for a moment, inspecting me, then added, indelicately, as they say, "You don't mind me being frank, you don't look as though you're exactly flush." He nodded, approvingly. "It's a rare thing to meet a man in your circumstances"—he gave a second once-over to my suit, which lacked an overcoat, though I have avoided telling you so because I did not wish to appeal to your compassion—"who wouldn't have spent a couple of days hanging on to that necklace, wondering what he might do with it. It's human nature. . . ."

"I have not always suffered my current and present reduced indisposition," says I to him in return, "but believe there is nothing more important in life than to be an honest gentleman, when circumstances do not interfere."

"Commendable," he said, shaking his head at the wayward-ness of the rest of the world, about which I could tell you a thing or two. "Commendable."

Now, as regards my relations with the police, which through no fault of my own have not always been amicable, this was something like the Bolshevik Revolution that took place some years ago in St. Petersburg, which I always thought had been in Florida.

Then Sergeant Scanlon came back in and took me out to the clean front room which the police present to the world, since their offices, such as they are, lack a woman's touch, and there's this guy standing there in a coat with a fur collar big as two mating muskrats hanging around his neck and a white scarf and a walking stick and a ritzy topper which he didn't remove, although a gentleman should always take off his hat when he comes in from the outside, though perhaps there are exceptions, especially if you are rich enough.

"This is Mr. Mulvaney himself," Sergeant Scanlon said. "Mr. Mulvaney, this is—"

"Bill Reardon," the fellow in the boiled shirt, who was wearing diamond studs twice the size of the rock in that ring in my pocket, which nobody seemed to miss, said to me before the sergeant could get the words out of his mouth. He stripped off a white glove and held out his hand, which I graciously accepted.

The detective nearly tripped over the two of us, interfering rudely, in his haste to produce the necklace for inspection, because the truth is that everybody wants credit, although the credit was entirely and obviously my own, but then a gentleman is not particular about such things, but lets those of lesser station, as they say, enjoy his bounty.

You could see clear enough how Mr. Reardon got rich, just as you could see the long foreign automobile with the driver in the monkey suit out by the curb, by the way he grabbed that necklace out of the lieutenant's hands, gave it a look as good as a tap with a jeweler's hammer, and shoved it into his overcoat pocket before you could say, "John Barrymore," who has always appeared to be a gentleman to me.

Then Mr. Reardon took his billfold out of the inside pocket of his overcoat, where my line of work informed me that he had put it because the dinner getup he had on for his party would not be cut for the accommodation of a big, fat wallet such as that, and he drew out a roll of bills that was not as impressive as some I have seen in my career but that certainly attracted my attention. And he started counting out twenties. When he got to the sum of one hundred dollars, he stopped and handed a portion of that size to me.

"Least I can do," he said. "Until the lawyers see about the reward. All has to be done up properly, of course." He smiled, as a true gentleman would under the circumstances, and said, "we'll just call this a tide-over. Won't come off the reward itself." Then he looked at me, once and then twice, with a serious mien, as they say, and said, "I hope you can use a thousand dollars, young man, since that's what you'll be getting."

"I was only doing my civical duty," says I.

"Well, I'm delighted to know that our town still has a few honest men on its streets," he said, with great approval.

I did not tell him I was originally from Scranton, although born in Nanticoke, but that is another story, since I thought it was only right to let him be proud of his town, besides he was counting out more money. He gave fifty dollars each to Sergeant Scanlon and to the detective, whose name appeared to be Derffler or something of that German nature, and they both said that, of course, they couldn't accept the money, although they took it in their hands, which were almost sweating, then Sergeant Scanlon said, "Well, Mr. Reardon, sir, I'll tell you what we'll do with these fruits of your fine generosity, and thank you, sir. We'll put them into the Police Benevolent Fund, won't we, Hank? And there they'll all go to good use, we'll see to it personally."

"Merry Christmas," Mr. Reardon wished us all, and he turned to go back out to his automobile, which was at least half a block long, and that was fine with me because now I had a hundred smackers in my pocket and a diamond ring besides and wasn't Annie going to be ashamed of herself? Oh, thou of little faith, as they say. Judge not, lest ye be judged.

But my release from the confining atmosphere of the police station house was not yet to be. Mr. Reardon turned to me once again and gave me the eagle eye like I was a pork roast he was considering buying at the butcher shop, for which purposes a swanky fellow like that has servants. And then my Christmas good fortune picked up again, for the deserving will get what they have coming, while the rest had better look out, as it says in the Bible.

"I'm a sorry excuse for a Christian," Mr. Reardon told us all. "And on this blessed eve, of all possible times. Young man—Mr. Mulvaney—if you have no pressing engagements, would you kindly join me for a bit? I have a number of out-of-town guests and I'd just like them to meet the kind of decent fellow Pottsville produces, say what they all might about King Coal and corruption and the breakdown of social order. It just might do them good, and remind them of the true spirit of Christmas."

※

You know," Mr. Reardon said, as we turned up Mahantango Street where the rich people of Pottsville live, almost all of them, in his automobile which smelled of leather and wax and

Mr. Reardon's cologne water and was as big inside as a hotel bedroom, at least in the hotels where my misfortune has sometimes required me to stay, "I've been looking around for a good man, someone to be something of a Man Friday for me. I don't mean that condescendingly, of course. But someone honest, whom I can trust to carry out sensitive . . . I won't say 'errands,' Mr. Mulvaney, since you might take it wrongly . . . but I need a man who can be relied upon. To put out fires, you might say."

"Fires," says I, "is my middle name, Mr. Reardon. And as it happens, I have only recently vacated my last instance of employment to seek my betterment elsewhere."

The perspicacious gentleman tugged off his right glove for the second time that evening, pulling on each finger, one after the other, then we shook hands again, and my good fortune of the evening seemed to me to have reached a climax, but how little I knew.

As we pulled up the drive, past all the fancy cars with their drivers out yakking with each other in the cold, I saw lights and heard music and knew this wasn't a tea party. There was a jazz orchestra playing the shimmy inside and you could have heard it over the mountain. The house was all lit up and packed as a bar on St. Paddy's. There even was a butler standing at the door, just standing there waiting like he had nothing but time on his hands, which always seemed a very gentlemanly way to do things to me.

Well, as I got out of the car, with the chaffeur, as they say, opening my door and the butler opening the door for Mr.

Reardon, I got a real gander at the size of the place, which was one of those dwellings of the finest quality that have more rooms than people, even if you count the servants, which I did not have time to do.

A young couple came out the front door giggling and all bent over like their raccoon coats were too heavy for their shoulders. They straightened up the moment they spotted Mr. Reardon, and if the doll didn't look like Constance Bennett, I don't know who does. The fellow, who had that college-boy, wiseacre look, apologized for leaving so early and told our host that it was a swell party, just swell, but they had a family commitment in Tamaqua, which Mr. Reardon didn't believe anymore than I did. Everybody said Merry Christmas, then off they went, those two. I bet I know what they had in mind, and she really did look like Constance Bennett, enough to break your heart, but that is none of my business, whatever they were going off to do, but I'd give you five to one it wasn't wrapping presents under the tree, but maybe some unwrapping, and a gentleman would say no more.

Mr. Reardon, who seemed to think of things one after the other, paused out of doors, which was getting colder by the minute, and said to me, right in front of the butler, though I pretended to think nothing of it, that he wished to offer me a suit of clothing, if I wouldn't be offended, since we were about the same size and build.

"Mr. Reardon," says I, "my recent fortunes, as you can see, have not been commensurate with the desires of my experience, so as a gentleman I could not offend your guests by the unfortunate condition of my suit, which has been ruined by the fire and my rescue of an innocent infant child and your necklace on Christmas Eve, of all possible nights, so I will not be offended in the least, and, as they say, if the suit fits, wear it."

"Harper," Mr. Reardon said to the butler, "take Mr. Mulvaney upstairs and see him outfitted." He turned to me again. "I had considered evening dress, but I suspect something of more utility might be the wiser choice—you won't mind putting in a brief appearance in a business suit, I hope? My guests will understand—I'll explain the entire affair while you're changing." He smiled, with what looked like all his own teeth. "Mrs. Reardon's going to be beside herself with happiness. Really, Mr. Mulvaney, you've made our Christmas. Harper, the new blue serge, I think, that just came up from Brooks. All the accoutrements and so forth."

"Very good, sir," said the butler, who was either English or on the con.

"You will excuse me, Mr. Mulvaney? For a few minutes? You'll be in the best of hands with Harper here."

And so I went upstairs, which was just full of loot and deserved better protection from the subordinate classes and their untoward ambitions. It was the classiest joint I ever saw and when the butler started laying out a shirt and tie I didn't want to embarrass him by pointing out that he seemed to be forgetting to set out a pair of shoes, so I picked out a swanky pair of two-tones, brown and white, that would make the eyes pop right out of every head in the Moose Lodge and Odd Fellows both, if you were a member, which I am not, though sometimes I have been a guest.

I washed the smoke and smut off my face and felt it my duty to splash cologne water on my hands then run it through my hair, for the benefit of my host and his guests. I was very glad that I had not skipped my bath the Saturday before, and that I have always taken care to wear undergarments you would not have to be ashamed of if you walked down the street in them at noon and had a soda at the Sun-Ray drugstore, but Harper, the butler, had such a snooty face to go with his high manners that I would have liked to tell him a thing or two, but did not want to interfere with the regulation of Mr. Reardon's domestic help, which was his problem.

I took care to palm the ring out of the butler's sight. In case he really was on the con.

Then down I went, dressed to the nines, to the hoolie, which was something else, the way rich people know how to do things and carry on like other people are afraid to. Mr. Reardon, who had been watching for me like a hawk, stopped the orchestra right in the middle of a tune, and the dancers all quit and looked around and he began the applause, which was, as they say, seconded. I guess he had told them all what a hero and man of remarkable honesty I am and have always meant to be, although life has not always been full of cooperation. Then I was introduced to everybody who was not dancing again and Mrs. Reardon was most profuse in her salutations, but, frankly, she was more than a little long in the tooth and I thought to myself, as a man of the world, that the old boy had something going on the side for sure, with all that money of his, but I will leave that to your imagination. For a minute, I thought she was going to kiss me, but she didn't, which was just as well, because her lips looked like two little pieces of liver and made me think again of Annie and how beauteous she is, at least as good-looking as Norma Shearer.

Now I do not wish to betray a confidence, which a gentleman must not do, but there was more booze at that party than on a rumrunner five miles offshore. Prohibition is not such a bad idea as people say, since not everybody can hold their liquor and, besides, there is good money to be made in it, but you would not have known it was the law of the land by the way the whisky and champagne wine were flowing at that party. Then Mr. Reardon took me into his study, as he called it, and introduced me to his two special guests, as he put it, which did not include the monsignor-looking church fellow, who might have been an Episcopalian anyway. The special guests were Senator Bridger and, of all people who would you think, Nicky the Taps Keough, who is not only of my own Irish persuasion but perhaps the biggest bootlegger and numbers man in eastern Pennsylvania, though he lives right in Pottsville, but the truth is I always stayed out of his way when he popped in the smoke shop or Sammy's Billiards, because he had an unforgiving reputation, as they say.

Senator Bridger was properly respectful of me, complimenting me on my honesty and my courage in rescuing the infant and so on. Nicky the Taps, who I called "Mr. Keough," of course, as any sensible man would, played along, but he had those wise-guy eyes which don't miss a trick, and I half expected him to reach into my pocket, pull out the diamond ring which no one had missed and which I had rescued from the fire, and ask me now where did that come from, Buster Brown? But he did not.

Mr. Reardon himself did the gentlemanly thing and went off to "refresh" as he said the drinks of the senator and Nicky the Taps, telling them he was leaving them in good hands, since I was now an employee of the Reardon Coal Company and don't try to hire me away. Well, Nicky the Taps didn't miss a trick, like I said, and no sooner is Mr. Reardon gone off to do his duty as a host than Nicky says to the senator, "Paul, if you don't mind, Mr. Mulvaney and I have something to discuss, entreenoo," as the French say, and the senator hightailed it out of there and didn't wait to be told twice. Then I thought, uh-oh, this is it. Jimmy Mulvaney, your luck has run out at last, but it was a good ride while it lasted.

But Nicky the Taps just gave me the up-and-down, a lot more businesslike and less Christmas in spirit than Mr. Reardon, and he said to me, "Mulvaney, I seen you around. Wouldn't you say?"

"Yes, Mr. Keough," says I. "An inopportune turn in my fortunes has—"

"Reardon's offered you a job?"

"Yes, sir, that he—"

"Then you got two jobs, right?"

"No, Mr. Keough, I'm afraid I am not presently em—"

He gave me a look to kill a marble statue stone dead and says, "I said now you got two jobs. Didn't I? Or didn't you hear what I said? You got one job working for Reardon, and another working for me. You're going to be my inside man, wherever Reardon has you traipsing around. Billy Reardon thinks he can trust you. But I happen to *know* I can trust you, isn't that right? Which I don't think I need to spell out in capital letters. Do I?"

"No, Mr. Keough."

He held out his hand, which was not as smooth as Mr. Reardon's, not by a long shot. "Well, then we got a deal. Between us micks, and you won't be sorry. And this is the last time I'm going to say this, Mulvaney: Whatever you been up to, this is my town. Now you're one of my boys. So leave the past behind, every inch of it, understand? And let me tell you something else. Also between us micks. I'm impressed by somebody smart enough to know his limitations. You knew you couldn't get rid of that necklace. I'm talking now, so you shut up and listen. I don't care how you came by it, whether you pulled it out of some burning baby's backside or out of the poor box. But you showed good judgment in getting rid of it, very good judgment." He smirked. "To the cops, of all things. That takes brass. That really takes the cake, I swear." He smiled, which somehow was not as reassuring as you would think. "You'll do okay, son, if you don't let your ambitions get ahead of your common sense." He let all that sink in, as they say, then added, "Merry Christmas. Now get out of here, before I get tired of looking at your dirty, bogtrotter mug."

Which I did.

I will tell you one last time, boy, that was a party. The young crowd, who acted as fast as they looked and danced like hopheads, thought I was quite a novelty, as they say. I didn't lack for a drink in my hand one minute, and it wasn't bathtub swill, either, and Julian English, the doctor's kid that has the car dealership when he's not drinking where every lowlife in town can take a gander at him, was already soused, but more of that later, since what really impressed me was his wife, Caroline, who was a looker like the dames that play society girls in the pictures. What she was doing with a drunk like young English I'll never know. Maybe his family had the simoleans. But money can't buy everything and Caroline English looked like a cat on the prowl and she wasn't hunting mice. I thought better you than me, Mister, 'cause she ain't going to hold still the minute you're not watching her. Maybe that was why he was drunk, who knows?

I didn't want to spoil Mr. Reardon's party after him being so responsible in his behavior toward me, but I noticed on the watch that somehow that I cannot explain appeared in the pocket of the vest of my suit, though I would have to buy a chain for it, that it was half past eleven almost, how time flew, and I didn't want to miss midnight mass, because Annie had her comeuppance in store for her, didn't she though, and she was going to get it where all the world could see.

I took my leave of Mr. Reardon and the missus, as they say, explaining that I never missed our midnight service on Christmas, which pleased Mr. Reardon no end and confirmed his judgment of me, while his wife, who looked like a dog's breakfast, no matter how many jewels she had hanging on her like a Christmas tree, said she'd always heard that Roman Catholic masses were enthralling at the high holidays. The little she knew.

As I was leaving, Mr. Reardon, who always seemed to think of things late, but better late than never, caught up with me at the door and pulled an overcoat, a real chesterfield, velvet collar and all, out of the closet without waiting for the butler to do it and draped it over my shoulders himself. I only hope it was one of his own coats, not one of the guests', but I suppose he could buy them a new one if they made trouble.

"I'm afraid we wouldn't be quite the same hat size," he said, "but just tell Robertson where to drop you and I'm sure you won't freeze. Merry Christmas, Mr. Mulvaney," and I said to myself it couldn't get any better than that.

Little did I know.

Robertson, the driver in the monkey suit, took me down the hill to the R.C. church, though the truth is I could have hoofed it nearly as fast as the time it took him, but I suppose he didn't want to damage that big Italian automobile as the street was icing over, and we pulled up in front of the place with me hoping Annie herself would be walking along just then to see me, but she wasn't, of course, because they all go early to get a seat and the place was packed. At least the steps weren't icy going up, because the shoes I had picked out were slippery.

A gentleman does not admit defeat in adversity, not that I was all that adverse at the moment, but I wanted Annie to see me, so though the church was crowded and standing room only, as they say, and the choir was honking louder than a pack of Methodists, I pushed up one side aisle, then down the other, then up the center, making like I didn't even see Annie sitting there with her jaw dropped like she was trying to sweep the floor with it, after calling me a bum and worse and questioning my honesty, when I had meant well all along and could not help it if the fight was rigged and nobody let on, what are friends for, I ask you?

I entered a pew up front, politely as a gentleman must do, and required an old cow to make room for me who was taking up two seats, at least. Annie could see me good, at least the back of my head, from where she was sitting, and I let her repent her ill words toward me without so much as turning around. Thank God, is all I can say, that I'd had a drink or two, though I wasn't counting, at Mr. Reardon's party, because there is nothing more boring on Christmas Eve, or Christmas morning, I should say, than religion, but I suppose that is part of it all and we must make allowances for the holidays.

Not that I did not try to pay attention, since I felt a new and deepened relationship, as they say, to Christmas, having just saved an infant child from certain destruction, but it was no good. I kept thinking about Annie, who I will admit I regarded as the true love destiny had prepared for me, despite her being of the Polish persuasion and having three brothers for whom Gorilla was too nice a name, but what do you expect of anybody dumb enough to go down in the mines and stay there?

I have always been a person to make the best of his circumstances and my period of military service, though it ended with misleading restraints placed upon my freedom, had taught me a thing or two about tactics. It would not have shined anybody's shoes for me to approach Annie right there, after the service, because she had not yet suffered enough for her lack of understanding, which she had displayed so cruelly toward me, as I have explained. And I knew how to torture her, don't think I didn't, because I study every single person who crosses my path, which is essential to my line of work. When the plate got passed around, I held one of those twenty dollars bills up to the light, the way a suspicious bank clerk eyeballs a watermark or a serial number, then dropped it in on top of all the nickels and quarters and a couple of dollar bills, people are cheap these days, even when they are getting rich on Wall Street.

As I went out, and none too soon, I got into the I-haven't-seen-you-at-mass-lately line at the door, just coughing distance ahead of Annie, and I put another twenty in Father Michael's own hand and surprised him like I was the Baby Jesus himself come strolling by. Normally, I don't believe in throwing good money after bad, but I knew I had another grand coming and I didn't think for a minute a gentleman like Mr. Reardon would go back on his word.

Well, out I go and I was feeling like a million bucks, not just a thousand, because it was cold and that chesterfield coat was warm as toast, like wearing a blanket that had been warming by the fire, and I could see half the congregation shivering around me and I didn't doubt they deserved it. Then I got the fright of my life, just about.

That detective, Derffler, and Sergeant Scanlon were standing right there at the foot of the steps, looking up at me.

I cursed myself up and down for not just giving them the ring with the necklace. Now I was in for it. I probably wouldn't even be able to angle that thousand-buck reward, which I had earned fair and square. I figured the best I could hope for was the first train out of town, so Mr. Reardon wouldn't be embarrassed and the police wouldn't, either, by their implied, as they say, misestimation of my character, which they would now see through different eyes and to my detriment.

I went down the steps, which were steep, as slowly as I could. I was just about ready to hold out my wrists for the cuffs, wondering if I shouldn't try handing them the ring first and telling them I was glad to see them because I'd forgotten all about it there in my pocket, when I saw they were smiling, but not the way cops do when they got you by the particulars.

"Ah, Mr. Mulvaney," the sergeant said, before that Dutchman detective could open his yap, "we was up to Mr. Reardon's looking for you, and he told me you'd come down here, God bless you, so down we came ourselves. We've got some good news for you, don't we, Hank?"

"Don't we ever," the detective said. "We thought you might be worried about that thief coming after you, the joker who stole the necklace. For revenge, you know. Well, we've caught him in the act. Breaking into Mr. Keough's smoke shop, which did not display very good judgment, if you know who Mr. Keough is. Anyway, when we explained things to him and produced the necklace, he broke down and confessed. He's singing like a bird."

"It didn't take more than a touch of the Irish to persuade him," Sergeant Scanlon added, "for he was a weak man, as thieves are like to be."

"It doesn't even look like you'll need to appear in court, Mr. Mulvaney. We've got all the confession we need. It's an open-and-shut case. All thanks to you."

"The newspaper lads have already been asking after you," the sergeant added, puffing out frozen breath like he was smoking two cigarettes at once, which reminded me I was overdue for a bout with a good cigar. "I've filled them in on the matter of the necklace, and they've spoken to Gracie Thomas about how you saved her and her baby both, but they'll still be wanting your photograph, sure as it's already Christmas Day in the morning. That's a handsome coat you've on, by the way. Christmas or no, Mr. Mulvaney, I believe you'll have the gentlemen of the press knocking on your door. And your address would be, by the way?"

I gave them Annie's address, since it was as good as mine. So to speak.

When the detective had gone on ahead, the sergeant nudged me off to the side, to let the last of the congregation pass us.

"Now, I'll be honest with you, Mr. Mulvaney," he said in a lowered tone. "I've had half an eye on you, these last few months. And I was not at all certain you were on the up-and-up, I wasn't. But I'm glad to see I was wrong, and I congratulate you on your good fortune. But success in life can bring a man complications, if he's not surrounded by friends who take an interest in his interests, if you have a mind to take some friendly advice. Now, Taffy Robertson whispered to me that Mr. Reardon's gone so far as to offer you a job, and I think I know what that job is, for I happened to know the larcenous fellow that last held the position, so let me explain something. There's things the public trust requires of those of us in the calling of law enforcement that would be hard for some of the public to understand. And there's times," he continued, "when a wise man turns a blind eye for the public good and simply accepts that an envelope will appear in his pocket at the end of the month. Am I making myself clear to you, Mr. Mulvaney, one honest Irishman to another?"

"Sergeant Scanlon," says I, "I have always supported the noble efforts of our police officers for the betterment of society, and I hope the police in our fair city of Pottsville will always know they can count on Jimmy Mulvaney. Through thick and thin."

"Ah, Mr. Mulvaney, you'll live to make your mother proud yet. Merry Christmas to you, then," and he gave me a wink and went off.

Well, you will understand that after an evening of such trials and tribulations, not to mention the sudden upturn, however deserved, in my personal fortunes, a fellow might feel the need for additional liquid sustenance, so I took myself down to Norwegian Street, to the Vereinhalle, which sounds German but isn't, at least not anymore, but is a speak where I have found companionship on many a lonely evening, until I decided it was time to go home to Annie. I thought I would permit those poor souls who might still be indulging their appetites that Christmas night to revel in the sight of me, as they say, and my new finery, though I promised myself I would not buy more than two rounds or spend more than ten dollars, which was plenty, because I had been warned that lawyers would be involved in the payment of my thousand-smacker reward and that could take forever.

I wondered if the first envelope of which Sergeant Scanlon had spoken would appear in my proverbial pocket at the end of that very month, in time for New Year's Eve, which I like to celebrate in a true and festive fashion, but have not always been able to honor according to my hopes and expectations.

Well, down I went to Norwegian Street, all innocent and unsuspecting and grateful for my good fortune, when what do I see a few doors down from the Vereinhalle but a trio of fellows beating and kicking the daylights out of a fourth individual who had recently embraced the sidewalk.

I strolled up to see if they needed any help, forgetting how respectable I had come to look in my fancy getup, and as soon as they saw me the three goons took off running, leaving the individual they had been chastising lying there on the sidewalk in an evening cape and a boiled shirt.

It was Julian English, the doc's boy, the one who had the looker for a wife. He was out cold, and his mug looked like he'd stuck it too close to the meat-grinder.

Now, I had enjoyed about as much excitement as I wished for one night and wanted only to distribute a few drinks among the neediest of my acquaintances downstairs in the Vereinhalle bar, and perhaps to say hello to a few of the girls whose profession it was to cheer up the customers, upon which I will not elaborate, as they say. But I could not leave the poor fellow on the sidewalk like that, considering that we had only just been introduced that very evening and he was something of a wheel in the community, though he liked to go slumming in pool halls, be that as it may. It occurred to me that yet another Christmas benefaction in which I played the role of the Good Samaritan might further cement my good name in the community, in addition to being the obligation of a gentleman, so I knelt down on his opera cape, to spare the knees of my new trousers, and inspected his corpus delecti to be sure he was still alive. Which he was.

The first thing I did was to remove the cash money from his billfold for safekeeping, in case the three assailants returned and, as they say, set upon him again. I was just putting the wallet back in his pocket when he groaned then bleated like a sheep. You can't be too quick, I thought. Well, he opened his eyes, one after the other, and drunk though he was, which I could tell by the fumes, since I could have lit a match and blown us both up, he recognized me, to my surprise and bewilderment, since we had only just exchanged names and he had been thumped pretty good.

"Jimmy," he said, clear as day, as if I was his long-lost brother, "Mulvaney . . ."

"That's me, Mr. English, you bet."

His eyes closed and he grunted again. "Not Mishter Englith," he said, "Jooliyun. *Joo*liyun . . ."

Then his eyes snapped open, as he remembered that he had not decided to take a nap on that sidewalk for his health.

"You rethcued me," he told me. "Did you rethcue me?"

"Well," says I, "it wasn't those six buckos who were pounding you halfway to China, now was it?"

"Sixuth?" he said. "Sixuth of them?"

It was my duty to illuminate his memory, as they say. "Maybe seven," I said. "I couldn't say for sure. There were more coming up behind you all the time. I just started swinging."

"Cowarths," he moaned.

"Well, now . . . I wouldn't go that far," says I. "They put up quite a struggle before I drove them off you." It would have been an insult to his conduct as a gentleman, if you see what I mean, to suggest that he had been knocked down on the sidewalk by cowards, and only by three of them, at that.

"You my fwiend. Jimmy Mulvaney. My fwiend. *Jimmeeee* . . . Mulvaney. Who rethcued mother and child. Rethcued me."

"Don't poke your teeth around with your tongue like that," says I, "or you'll lose them sure. You got to let them settle."

He closed his eyes again.

"Cawoline going to be *tho* mad . . . only wantet a drink . . . nobody my fwiend anymore . . . all alone . . . no fwiend . . ."

"Except Jimmy Mulvaney."

". . . Jimmy Mulvaney . . ."

"Here. Sit up now. Spit out the blood before you choke on it."

I helped him lift himself up off the sidewalk, which was all muck and blood by the looks of it, though it was hard to see much in the space between the streetlamps. He spit a few clots of blood toward the curb, but no teeth.

"Go home now," he said, unsteady as a two-timing woman.

Well, it was clearly my duty to help the poor chump get home, which I set about doing, forgoing my anticipated pleasure of a Christmas celebration in the company of my friends, some of whom I suspected had just beaten Julian English to a pulp, not that I'm saying they may not have had their reasons.

I finally made out that he and that doll of his lived in one of the fancy town houses down toward the end of Centre Street, which was a pretty good address for the better classes starting out in life, and I got him to his door after a great deal of effort and danger on my part, most of which consisted of preventing him from getting blood all over my new chesterfield coat.

There was a light burning in the entryway, so young English hadn't been given the boot, I didn't think. But he had mislaid his key in the course of the evening, so I was forced to disturb the slumbers of the household by ringing the bell. Then I knocked. Then I rang the bell again. And knocked again. Until finally that high-class looker of a wife of his, not a servant, opened the door in her nightgown, which wasn't made of sackcloth and ashes, let me tell you. She must have thought it was her husband and nobody else banging on the door, but I didn't complain.

"My God," she said, looking at the mug on him.

"He'll be all right, Mrs. English," says I. "He only needs to sleep it off and lay off his front teeth until they settle in again. A month from now, you won't notice the difference."

Maybe the rich are all like Mr. Reardon, noticing things late. But it was only when I finished speaking that Caroline English, who looked like Gloria Swanson all over again, noticed that I was not only standing in her doorway but holding up her husband.

"Oh, Mr. Mulvaney," she said, not batting an eyelash, that's how they are, "you seem to be the hero of everybody's evening. Where did you scrape up this drunken *sot* of a husband of mine?"

Scraped up is right, I almost told her.

"He was involved in an altercation," says I. "I was just strolling by and became aware of his predicament, as they say."

At that, Julian English began to york all over the place. I did my best to turn him toward the front stoop and away from the carpet, but a man must have his priorities in life and I figured the Englishes could afford a new carpet runner quicker than I could afford a new chesterfield overcoat.

"Merry Chrithmus," Julian English said, when he had delivered all his goods.

"Oh, God," Mrs. English said. "Mr. Mulvaney . . . I *hate* to impose upon you further . . . but could you—please—help me get this *sot* upstairs?"

We both of us got under an arm and dragged him toward the staircase. I tried to tilt him so that any further gushers would go her way, not mine. I did debate with myself as to the gentlemanly quality of such conduct before realizing that I was already doing the lady of the house such a favor that it would place her too much in my debt if her husband were to vomit on my new coat, which was a pricey number by the feel of it.

The stairs were narrow and I went up first, dragging the dumb lug and telling myself that if I was married to that dame of his, I'd come home standing up every which way, not falling down and passing the beef stew. I thought he was going to grace us with another gift when he opened his mouth, but he only started singing, "Deck the halls with boughs of holly," and Mrs. English said, "Thank God, the servants are off for Christmas."

We dumped him on a bed and he started snoring right away. I almost told her that he should lay on his stomach, not his back, so as not to choke to death if he started speaking in tongues again, but I figured that was her business.

"You look like you could use a drink," she said, still in that nightgown.

"I'm not usually a drinking man," says I, with a pitying look in the direction of her husband. "Two's my limit." Which was not strictly true, but I thought it might help reassure her if I was to offer a moral example at a time when she might have become disillusioned with the male race, which would have been a waste of some very fine horseflesh.

"How many have you had tonight?" she asked, bold as brass.

"Two," says I. "But that was before midnight, so I'm counting for a new day."

"You won't mind if I join you?" she asked me, like we were in a fancy play on the stage and had just come in, la-de-da, from tennis or something.

She led me downstairs, where there was a Christmas tree with no end of presents underneath, though they didn't seem to have any kids, and she mixed up two Canadians and water, and she didn't spare the poison. More to my surprise, since I recognize a lady when I see one, she knocked hers right back and poured herself another like she was standing on the Ford assembly line. Then she took my coat off my shoulders with a laugh, as if we were old friends for a hundred years.

"Help yourself," she told me. "I've got to go to the powder room for a moment."

Now, I believe that human prosperity should be shared out, and after she told me to help myself and shut herself in the can, I gave the Christmas presents under the tree the once-over, since I was owed something for my troubles, if we are to be honest, and if it wasn't for me Julian English might have froze to death in the street, if the temperature had dropped a little.

Greed is not one of the characteristics of the gentleman, so I just poked through the smaller presents, the ones that said To Caroline, From Ju, until I found one just the right size and shook it by my ear. It sounded like perfume, all right, which I thought would be advantageous when I returned to forgive Annie for her behavior the evening before. I slipped it in the pocket of my chesterfield, which lay over the back of a stuffed chair, then, since Mrs. English had decided to take her own good time in the pot, I had a quick look through the presents that said From C., To J., and picked out a little box I suspected of harboring a wristwatch, which young English, through his bad behavior, would only have lost or broken or given away to a woman of the worst sort under the influence of alcohol, whereas it was a small token for my helpful conduct and my despoiled, as they say, evening.

She was quiet as a cat and nearly surprised me before I had the ticker hidden in my coat pocket, but she didn't see a thing because she went straight for the booze on the little trolley, knocked back number three, flopped down on the sofa by the tree, and said, "Mr. Mulvaney . . . I'm inex*press*ibly embarrassed . . . and hope I may count on you, as a gentleman, to keep our little secret." She gestured, not with a lot of juice in it, toward her husband upstairs. Then she stretched out a little longer on the cushions and said, "How shall I ever thank you?"

❊

I will leave the rest to your imagination, but I will tell you that whoever the guy was who said the rich are different didn't know what he was talking about. She didn't have a brain in her head, no more than her husband did, when it came to respectable behavior, but I had no intention of soiling a lady's reputation, as they say, and I got out of there before dawn and paid attention to anybody who might be watching. You have to think of others at a time like that.

Well, the thing with Annie is she doesn't like to be woke up unexpected, and after midnight mass I knew she'd be sleeping, if her conscience wasn't keeping her awake, which it should have been. So I walked all the way up Centre Street to see if the Coney was open on Christmas and it was, so I had ham and eggs and toast and more ham after, since I was flush and hadn't even had to pay for my drinks or those of my companions I didn't see, since I never made it to the Vereinhalle but took my refreshment at the abode of Mr. and Mrs. English, as they say.

When I pulled out Andy Jackson, the waitress, who was named Sally and wouldn't have been so bad except for a brown wart with hair by her nose, which I did not find lady-like, said, "Who're you all of a sudden, J.P. Morgan? Yesterday, you was nursing a cup of coffee for two hours and picking the scraps off the tables when you thought I wasn't looking. Now I'm supposed to break a twenty on Christmas morning, go on with you."

I very nearly told Sally to keep the change, and might have done so in the generous capacity of my heart, but that wart prevented the gesture from being classified as a sound investment in the future, so I pointed out that I was standing there offering to pay my bill and couldn't help it if she couldn't make change, could I? She told me to beat it and I said I would come back the next day, when I hoped the cash register would be more affluent.

I was halfway down the block when I remembered that my pockets also contained a sum I was holding in security for Julian English and that some of said money might have been applied toward payment for my breakfast, if smaller bills were involved. I stopped in my tracks and counted out thirty-seven dollars that I had rescued from his assailants, which seemed a pretty shabby amount for him to be carrying around on Christmas Eve, considering how the Englishes liked to put on the dog. I also realized that, if I went back to the Coney so soon to pay that bill, my gesture might be misunderstood, since I had only just insisted I had nothing smaller than a twenty and did not want to appear dishonest. So I kept walking.

Now, I am robust by nature and attentive to my health, but the events of the past twelve hours had been a drain upon my energies. I wanted to sleep so I might enjoy my reconciliation with Annie in an appropriate manner, so to speak. So I went down to the new hotel, the Necho, where the riffraff doesn't even get in the front door, and I laid out six bucks for a fancy room and had the bellboy bring up a razor and shaving soap. He was unhappy about working on Christmas morning, even though that was his job, so I tipped the kid a buck, which Julian English could easily afford.

The truth is that I couldn't sleep, only two hours. I was anxious to see Annie and had begun to entertain the fear that she would go off to Shenandoah, although her brothers had threatened to kill her for her public and intimate association with me, of which her family did not approve, so I took a hot bath, just for her, and shaved until you would have thought my cheeks were a baby's in the dark. I checked out, tipping the desk clerk, too, until the total was almost nine dollars and never was money better spent, since I looked more like Ronald Colman than ever, which I have been told on more than one occasion, and I remembered that the representatives of the press were expected to pay a call, previous to which Annie and I had unfinished business.

Walking up the street, I felt like a million bucks. It was Christmas, after all, and I had finally discovered the luck that I deserved, which does not come to everyone, since some people are unlucky all their lives. I knocked on the front door until Mrs. Seligman, who knew a good deal when she saw one, finally came out and let me in, since Annie wasn't about to come down, or so it would appear. Fortunately, I had given Mrs. Seligman a good tip more than once on a horse or two, and she liked to play the ponies, though they don't run on Christmas, for reverent reasons.

Up the stairs to Annie's dwelling of residence I went, with my heart pounding, as they say, for I had learned my lesson, which Mrs. English had given me and I will say no more, that I was in love with Annie as if I had stars in my eyes the size of medicine balls.

The object of my affections opened the door after I had knocked for about ten minutes, looked me over through the crack with the chain still hooked, and said, "What'd you do, rob a bank?"

"I told you my ship was going to come in."

"Well, you can sail right back off in it," she said, though I could tell she didn't really mean it.

I reached into my pocket for the bottle of perfume that was all wrapped up and my good fortune continued, for I realized at the last moment that I had not had the good manners and foresight to separate the little card directing the gift to Caroline English, from her husband, which I did in my pocket before I produced the present.

"Here," says I. "Merry Christmas. A special something for my special girl. Unless you don't want it, perhaps?"

Now, you might say that I am by nature a gambling man, although it is untrue, since I only bet on a sure thing, to the best of my knowledge, but I recognized that I was taking a risk, since there was always a chance that there wouldn't be perfume in that package at all, but God only knew what. But a man must be bold in life, or he doesn't get anywhere.

Before she would accept my gift, which was from the heart, if ever a gift was, she said, "If you're so flush all of a sudden, what about the money you took out of my drawer, what about that, huh? You hit the numbers or something, you chiseling mick?"

"Annie, my dearest darling, my rose," says I, "there appears to be a distressing instance of misunderstanding between us, as they say. I never took a penny out of your drawers, I didn't, not one red cent," which was true in a manner of speaking, since I hadn't touched the jar of pennies she kept, which seemed beneath the dignity of a gentleman. "I have my good friend Sergeant Scanlon of the police department looking into the theft this very minute."

"You don't even know Tubby Scanlon, who're you kidding?"

"Wait and see, my dearest, wait and see. There is much

about me what you do not know. Meanwhile, how much did that criminal take from your store of treasure, as they say?"

"Twenty-six bucks, and you know it as well as I do."

Her temper was softening by the minute, and I intended to do all I could to inspire her better nature. So I took out my reserve of banknotes, all of which I had consolidated in the interests of security, and generously peeled off two tens and two fives, which I did not think Julian English would begrudge me, under the circumstances.

"Here," says I, "you can pay me back when the police arrest the thief and return your rightful money to you." Then it occurred to me that I was being ungallant and that the police would not be returning any money, anyway, so I added, "I mean, you don't have to return it at all. Consider it my contribution to the welfare of our household."

"And long overdue, you ask me." Her voice was almost sweet.

I offered her the present once again, which she took, then she closed the door and undid the chain and let me in, though not without foreboding and, as they say, castigation in her eyes, which are gorgeous as Dolores del Rio's.

Annie sat by the little Christmas tree she had set up on a table between the Victrola and my chair and opened up her gift without further ado. It warmed my heart to observe her. A gentleman should always give a lady gifts, although he is not always in a position to do so.

Fortunately, young English was a sensible man and had chosen a perfume of real top quality, as you could see by the bottle.

Annie began to cry, which women like to do when they are enjoying themselves at a man's expense. "All my life," she said, "all my life, I've wanted a bottle of this, all my life."

"The first of many," says I.

All of a sudden, her face got on this frightened look that would have broke the heart of a born criminal. "Jimmy," she said, through her tears and her sniffling, "Jimmy, you ain't been up to anything crooked, have you? Please tell me you ain't been doing anything crooked, would you, please?"

"My dearest darling," says I, "you are looking at a man who has been recognized for his intricate values, as they say, and who has been begged to accept an executive position with Mr. Reardon and his coal company, that's Mr. William Reardon of Mahantango Street, in case you don't know, and I have generously accepted. From now on, there will be a paycheck coming in regularly of a size that will allow me to treat you as I have always said I would do someday, but you were impatient with my efforts, oh ye of little faith. . . ."

I did not mention the two other jobs, with Nicky the Taps and assisting the police, which I was not entirely certain were unrelated to each other. Anyway I have never thought it gentlemanly to bother a lady with mathematical questions, and what Annie didn't know wouldn't hurt her.

She beamed like a kid, just like a little kid. Then she jumped up and threw her arms around me. If I was a more sensible man and less softhearted, I would have left it at that, having enjoyed the finest Christmas of my life and perhaps in all of history, at least in recent years, but, no, I couldn't leave well enough alone, could I?

I pulled out the diamond ring, which was of the engagement sort.

"Merry Christmas," says I.

With a Christmas toast to the spirit of John O'Hara

In Every Inn

In every inn in Bethlehem
The owner loves a census.
It fills his rooms with travelers
Wary of offenses.

Kitchens swarm, the wine runs out,
Dubious women appear.
Business is splendid, the till is full.
It's the fat time of the year.

What an annoyance they *must have been,*
That old man and his bride—
Her as pregnant as a sow
And patched on every side.

An innkeeper let them rest in his barn
And got no sleep on Christmas morn.

The Christmas Joe

※

Christmas Eve, 1933

Betty Marzinski knew what was going to happen. As soon as the girl laid down her baby and got up from the booth, she knew. Betty continued cleaning the grounds from the coffee urn, but she had learned how to watch without watching. And to listen. She couldn't hear what the girl whispered to the truck driver at the counter, but she saw one of his eyebrows go up. The girl rested her hand on the driver's shoulder. Just for a couple of seconds. The trucker lowered his mug and turned his head to give the girl the once-over.

The girl was back in the booth, cradling her infant in her arms, when the joe who had brought them in came out from the gents', shaking the last drops of water from his hands. That told Betty he was all right. No prize, but all right. He washed his hands, but wouldn't dry them on the dirty rag of a towel. He wasn't any prime specimen, but a man who kept himself clean when he was down wasn't a bum.

And the poor sap was down. Anybody could see that. Not just by the wear on his clothes. The bent shoulders and the whipped look in his eyes said, "No job." He was a big man, a workingman, but he didn't look like a dummy. His face was intelligent, though there was something foolish in it, too.

Betty knew what was going to happen, and it wasn't right. But it wasn't her business. Not yet.

"Yo, Garbo," the trucker called. "How's about my bill?"

Betty, who did not look like Garbo and knew it, turned her hardening eyes on him, one hand on her hip.

"I thought you wanted fresh coffee? The fuss you made." She knew very well that the trucker no longer wanted his mug refilled, but she felt a need to give it to him just a little. For what he was going to do. Even though she wanted him to leave now, as badly as he wanted to go.

"I changed my mind. I'm running late."

"Christmas Eve," Betty said, still needling the guy, "I guess you want to get home to your family."

If looks could kill. Well, he had it coming. Little guy, all puffed up in the chest, with no moxie behind it. He wasn't going to get half what he thought he was off of that girl, with her glad rags that wanted to be fancy but just looked cheap. The fabric told you all you needed to know, flashy not quality. With a seamstress for a mother, Betty had grown up knowing cloth by sight. For what good it did her. But the trucker was in for a lot less of a Christmas present than he thought he was going to get. Unless he was one of the rough ones. Then the girl might get a surprise herself.

"I got no family," the trucker said, walking over to the register, where a pasteboard Santa waved a pasteboard bell. "No more than you do."

"How do you know I got no family, buster?"

"You got no ring. And you don't got the look."

"The little you know. That's sixty-five cents."

The trucker pulled out a roll of bills for all the world to see. Although, this late, the world consisted only of Betty, the couple in the booth with the infant, and Smitty flopped on his chair back in the kitchen, glad to be cooking nothing. The trucker's roll looked fat enough. But Betty would have laid down good money that it was nothing but ones, maybe a five or two. The trucker was that kind of guy. Out to fool the world. And too dumb to see the world was fooling him.

When Betty started counting out his change, the trucker said, "Keep it, sister. Merry Christmas." Putting on the dog for the girl in the booth.

Betty gathered up the coins and held them out.

"You're going to need it more than me," she told him.

He wouldn't take his change, so Betty slapped the silver down on the counter. Glaring at the guy. With the eyes she herself could feel hardening as the months turned into a year and kept slumping along, like beat-down men in a soup line. His doings were none of her business—not yet—but she always had a temper on her.

"Send it to Roosevelt," the trucker said. He dropped his cap on his head, turned up the collar of his jacket, and went out into the raw night.

Betty let the coins lie. Later. Sure. She'd take them. Better than leaving them for Smitty to grab when he came out from the back to lock things up. Smitty got paid enough. And he did enough grabbing. For all the good it did him.

She heard the truck start up and pull out.

The man in the booth glanced out at the noise. Natural thing to do. But the girl was careful not to look through the window. She was all smiles now, making nice with the poor sap across the table from her. Betty knew the kind. And she despised them. From way down deep.

But she didn't say a word when the girl handed the baby to the guy who had let her order a meatloaf dinner while he settled for a cup of coffee and a piece of the bread that came with the girl's meal. Seeing that, Betty had brought them another plate of bread. Mr. Salvatore was stricter than ever about portions, but old Sal wasn't in, and he wasn't going to come in on Christmas Eve. The wops were big on family and going to church, worse than the Hunkies up home. Mr. Salvatore wasn't going to know a thing, and what he didn't know wasn't going to hurt him. Besides, the bread would be stale when they opened back up the day after Christmas. And the guy was hungry. It was on his face plain as dirt.

And Smitty wasn't paying attention, not that she cared. He didn't make any noise about things out front. He just fried up the orders Betty called through to him. Then he sat back down on his fat behind and paged through *The Police Gazette* or some other crummy rag. Scratching himself and moving his lips while he read. She could have lifted the till and been halfway to Jersey before he noticed anything.

Betty didn't know whether to be sorry about the extra portion of bread or not, given what was going on now. The whole thing made her mad. Mad enough to start yelling. But she just wiped down the pie case and let things play out. Because she saw more than any of them. How it was going to be in the end. She was mad now, because of the way people were. But they were all doing her a favor. She saw it so clearly it was hard to keep her mouth shut. She hated what they were doing, but she wished they would hurry up and and get it done.

Without making it obvious, Betty watched the man, the girl, and the baby. The girl was all smiles now, though she had been sour and full of mouth when they came in. Once she got the kid stuffed into her joe's big arms, she gave the poor sap a peck on the forehead, just at the hairline, flirting, and said, loud as if she was on a stage, "Girlie business. Don't you go getting impatient with me now."

Halfway down to the end of the diner, she turned to flash a smile, wiggling her fingers in a wave like she'd seen in some movie. The girl was so set on convincing the guy in the booth that she couldn't get enough of him that she almost walked into the tree with the lights and the dime-store balls and last year's tinsel.

When the door that led to the cans swung shut, Betty took the pot of fresh coffee over to the booth.

"You want another fill-up?" she asked the guy. He held the baby like it was a loaded gun and he didn't like guns.

"I thought you said we only got one refill?"

Betty shrugged. "It's Christmas Eve. Nobody else ain't coming in. I'd just have to throw it away."

His eyes narrowed. Just a little. "I don't take charity, miss."

Betty stepped back. "Buddy, I'm offering you a cup of coffee. Not a Christmas box from the Salvation Army. You want a refill or not?"

Cautiously, he separated one hand from the baby and slid his cup toward her. "Sure. Thanks. I didn't mean nothing."

Out in the blow, the girl was carefully, quietly, lifting a suitcase from the old Ford the three of them had driven up in. Betty pretended not to see a thing.

"Don't worry about it. Nobody's exactly got the Christmas spirit around here."

"Don't get me started," he said. "Listen, you don't mind my asking. Why were you so tough on that trucker? He just tried to tip you. I mean, jeez . . ."

"Some tips I don't need."

"He was just a working stiff, like the rest of us. He done something to you, you should've said something. I could've taken care of him, if he was up to something."

Betty saw the girl, loaded down with a suitcase and a hatbox, struggling along the street. In the snapping rain. To where the trucker would be waiting.

"Looks to me like you got your hands full," Betty said, drawing his eyes down to the baby. "Boy or a girl?"

She noticed that he had to think before answering.

"A boy," he said.

"Yeah? What's his name?"

Again, he had to think an instant too long. "Dougie. Douglas."

"Like Douglas Fairbanks?"

"I guess."

"Your wife's a looker, though," Betty told him, "I'll say that." Although she knew the girl was not the man's wife. She had to keep the conversation going, to give the girl time to make it down the street, climb into the cab of the truck with all her belongings, and get away. Even though she felt no least sympathy with the little bum. Not one shred. Betty didn't even like the way she looked, though she had the kind of looks that most men went for.

"Well, to tell you the truth, she's not my wife exactly." He smiled. Almost. The guy didn't look like he had a full smile left in him. "She's okay, though. She's a good kid. Just got some tough breaks, is all. It's the times."

The baby began to cry. The man looked lost all of a sudden. He wasn't really stupid, but he wasn't quick, either. That was for sure. He wasn't going to win any radio quiz shows. The infant's cry sharpened into a scream.

"Give me the kid for a minute, you want to?" Betty said.

The guy didn't need to be asked twice. He held out the baby instantly. "I'm no good with kids," he said. "Never was."

"You married? Before, I mean?"

He shook his head. "Should've been. You know how it is. Somebody just lets you down. When you're counting on them. All most people think about is money nowadays." He raised his eyes, almost meeting hers. "It's the capitalist system. The system ain't no good, it ruins people. You know how it is, working like you got to work in here. I bet you seen it all."

Yes. She knew how it was. Though she hadn't seen it all. At least not yet. She knew what happened to the miners up home when they lost their work, then their pride, then their homes. Kids in rags and eating government surplus. When they could get it. Sleeping under hand-out army blankets that smelled of disinfectant and BO. She knew what she had lost herself. But Betty also knew enough of the world to know she hadn't seen it all, not by a long shot. And she didn't want to see it, either.

She laid the baby against her shoulder and shuddered. Almost as if a man had touched her someplace where he shouldn't have. But the infant quieted down.

"You're pretty good with kids," the guy in the booth said. As if he'd seen some kind of miracle.

"Big family," Betty told him. But her attention had shifted away, toward the infant.

"Know what?" the guy said. "You're smiling. No offense, but that's the first time all night I seen you smile."

At once, her smile tightened, though it did not disappear. She cast a wiseacre look down the length of the diner. Toward the tree. And the swinging door that led to the ladies' and gents'. There wasn't a hint of motion in that door, and there wasn't going to be. Betty wondered if the girl had managed to jack the back door open, or if she had just climbed out the window. They kept the window locked and barred in the gents, to make it tougher for the deadbeats, but Sal wouldn't lock the women in. He was moony about women, tightwad that he was, convinced that every one of them was a chip off the Virgin Mary. The way Catholic men were. Even her old man had a touch of that, though it hadn't stopped him from smacking the daylights out of her mother when he came home drunk or when the shifts were cut back and he had time on his hands. Well, she knew better. It wasn't just the men. You couldn't even trust a nun, not the half of them.

"What do *you* see I should be smiling about, anyway?" Betty asked, not caring if the guy answered.

"Jeez," he said, ignoring Betty and her question. "Margie's been in there a while, though."

"Women got things to take care of men don't," Betty told him. Quickly. With fear running down through her, a warning as shrill as a colliery whistle. She had to give that little tramp plenty of time to get away. Time, and extra time.

"Here," she said, passing back the infant. Before it got too hard to do it. "Just don't hold him so flat like you were doing. You got to keep his head up higher."

As she handed the baby over, she smelled the guy. He needed a wash. Not that he was the only one in the country who did.

She began to turn away.

"Hey," the poor joker said. "You don't mind, how's about a refill for Margie, too? Before we hit the road?"

Without a word, Betty extended the pot toward the cup on the other side of the table.

"Not too full," the guy said. "She takes milk."

"That kid ate anything?" Betty asked suddenly, alarmed again. She was jumpy as a thief with one hand in the poor box. She didn't know what she'd do, if the baby hadn't been fed. One thing she didn't have behind the counter was a bottle with a nipple on it.

The guy reddened. "She fed him. In the car. Before we come in. She didn't want to make a show."

"Listen," Betty said. "We got some pie left. It's only going to go to waste. We ain't even open tomorrow. We got cherry and punkin. . . ."

The guy looked at her. "Where you from, anyway?"

"What do you mean, where am I from? Where are *you* from?"

"Up Mahanoy City," he said. "You? You sound like you cracked some coal yourself."

"Not me," she lied. "I was born right here. In Reading, Pee-yay. I got nothing to do with them yonkos. And I ain't no coalcracker."

He shrugged. "Well, I guess I'm not, either. Not anymore. I been down at Bet'lem Steel since I was sixteen. All the good that did me. Twelve years. Best union man on the floor. All the good it did me. They gave me the bum's rush last summer. Me, and eight hundred other guys."

"I read about that. They were laying off here, too," she said, glad she had turned the conversation away from her place of birth. "At least, they were laying off the ones who weren't laid off already. Punkin or cherry?"

He looked at her. As if he already knew. With a whole lifetime of sadness in his eyes. But he didn't know. Not yet.

"As long as it ain't no charity. Cherry. For both of us." Then he added, "Please."

"Whipped cream on it? Hold the kid up higher, like. Against your shoulder."

"Sure. Whipped cream on both, you don't mind. I wasn't just laid off. I got canned. For sticking up for working stiffs like you and me."

Betty ignored the invitation to talk about how tough things were. She'd heard every complaint a hundred times over. She wasn't mean. At least she didn't think so. She felt sorry enough for the poor joes who went in and out the door of the diner. She didn't say a word when a guy emptied the sugar container into his water glass or palmed the leftovers from the next table. But she couldn't remember a time when life hadn't been tough. The coal towns weren't exactly dripping with furs and diamonds. You grew up hard. If you lasted long enough to grow up at all. The rest of them were just learning what it was like.

Betty cut two big portions of cherry pie, then stirred up the cream from the icebox and spooned it out. Glancing through the narrow service window into the kitchen now and then. Checking. She couldn't see Smitty's face. But she saw that his paper had fallen to the floor and his hands lay in his lap. Snoozing.

When she set down the two pieces of pie, the poor sap asked, "Do you think you could go in back, you don't mind? And see if Margie's okay? She never takes this long."

Betty shrugged. "It's not like I'm loaded with customers, I guess."

"Christmas Eve, up where I come from," the guy said, "all the diners are packed. Standing room only. Just packed. Specially later on, after the midnight mass lets out. Not that religion's worth a damn, I don't mean. It just keeps the people fooled and quiet, so's they can be exploited. But after midnight mass is when all the drunks come in for something to eat. There's one in Frackville stays open all night. Just for the drunks."

"Well, we don't serve no drunks here," Betty said. "And I don't know nothing about the coal towns. And I don't want to know."

"It's a different world up there," he said. Then he made a face. "I guess I should've gone down the mines, like my pop. But I seen what it did to him." He snorted. Like a man broken down, played out, kept in one piece by nothing but memories. He wasn't much over thirty. Not even that. Not if he worked for Bethlehem Steel for twelve years, starting at sixteen, and only lost his job the summer before. Twenty-eight. Or twenty-nine. Six or seven years older than her. And already kicked so hard he might not get up again. Of course, she had a job. That helped. She had seen what being out of work did to men. Took all their pride away. Then it started taking the rest of them. Until there was nothing left but their big mouths and their fists.

"You're lucky you got a job," he said, reading her mind.

"Yeah. Don't I know it?"

"And you can eat. All you want, I guess."

"The boss watches. He's Italian, they're like that. He keeps count of everything. Anybody runs out the door without paying, I get docked."

"But you got a job. Say, would you check on Margie, though? The kid might be sick or something. Tell you the truth, that's the only meal she ate all day."

Betty turned away. Toward the tree. And the swinging door that led back to the cans. It was all right now. The girl was long gone. Probably past Hamburg, if they were headed north. And they had a good head start to Philly, if they were going in the other direction. Not that Betty thought the sad sack in the booth would have the gumption to go after her.

She just slipped through the door, paused for one breath, and hurried back out into the smells of cigarette smoke, coffee grounds, and grease. Before the guy could empty the register and disappear on her. In case the whole thing was one big put-up job, with all of them in on it. You couldn't trust anybody anymore. Everything was all broken down, and you couldn't even begin to tell who was on the up-and up by looking at them. Or even by talking to them. They all had plenty in the mouth, but nothing in the pocket. The more beat down they got, the bigger the deal they had to pretend to be. Every one of them going someplace where a big job was waiting, just for him. The big, rock-candy mountain. Once, she had needed to hold the pie knife against the throat of a man in a nice suit and tie until Smitty got up off his behind and came out from the kitchen with the shotgun. Mr. Banker or Mr. Lawyer. With his hand in the till of a greasy spoon a mile outside of Reading.

Before she said one word out loud, Betty prayed, quickly, to the God she had turned away from two years before. After He turned away from her and the baby.

The guy in the booth must have been a born sucker. He didn't get it. Even now.

"She's gone," Betty said. From two booths away. In case the guy threw a fit or something. "She must've gone out the back door, broke it open."

For a second, she thought he was going to drop the kid on the linoleum.

"What do you mean, she's gone?"

"I mean she's gone, is what I said. Go look for yourself."

He laid the baby right on top of the table, between the pieces of pie, without even pretending to be gentle about it. He ran back into the ladies' and then checked the gents', too. Cursing and making sounds like a half-killed animal. Then he ran outside, into the slop of the night, without his coat or hat.

Betty lifted the baby from the clutter of the tabletop. Before it could do any damage. Or make itself any dirtier than it was. As soon as she picked it up, the infant emptied its bowels.

When the guy came back inside, with his hair wet and his shoulders soaked, he had the look of someone who just found out about a death in the family. Close in the family. But he wasn't crying. That was something.

He didn't say a word. Just sat back down in the booth, picked up his fork, touched it against the remnants of the pie, and froze up.

Betty rocked the baby against her. She had smelled plenty worse.

"Hey," she said. "Buddy."

The man did not look up.

"Mister. You. Whatever your troubles, I'm sorry for them. But this baby needs its diapers changed. You got any clean diapers out in your car?"

"I don't know," he said. Voice flat as a penny left on a train rail.

"Well, could you go look, do you think? I can't have the place smelling like this."

Surprisingly, obediently, he got back up. This time, he put on his coat and his browned-off hat before he went outside. Betty watched him through the window, with the pink electric sign reflecting off the puddles and the ice. When she saw him climb into the car, it occurred to her that the guy might drive right off. But she realized, even before he reappeared from inside the vehicle, that it wasn't going to go like that. With every passing second, she saw more clearly how things were going to be. The way she wanted it to be.

Bobby Reese had promised to marry her. And she had been dumb enough to believe him. Her father had forbidden her to go anywhere near Bobby early on, since he was a Protestant and the mine superintendent's son. But she hadn't listened. Even when her mother had the priest talk to her. Father Dilenko hadn't preached. There was no God or religion, or even right or wrong, in what he said. He just told her, cold as a lump of coal in the dead of winter, that the son of Robert J. Reese was not going to marry a company-house Polish girl whose parents were just off the boat. That was just the way things were. She was throwing herself away, getting a reputation and maybe worse, and spoiling her chances of finding a decent husband.

The priest had been right. She had thrown herself away. When she came up unlucky, Bobby Reese accused her of sleeping with half the Hunkies in Coaldale and Lansford. And a quarter of the micks, too. Even though he had been her only one, her only love, and he damn well knew it.

Her mother had talked to her, with the old country habits poisoning every word, telling her that Mrs. Yursavage up the hill would take care of everything, if Betty just shut her mouth and didn't let on that anything had happened.

But Betty would not go to Mrs. Yursavage, even though her father beat her bloody.

She had the child in a Catholic home, in Allentown. It died in less than two days. She hadn't even tried to go home after that. The sisters found her work as a housemaid, but the man of the house knew too much, or figured out too much, and wouldn't let her alone. When she threatened to tell his wife, he stole the pay she'd been saving in a sock and told her to get out before he killed her. She made it as far as Reading on what she had in her handbag, worried half to death that she was going to turn into one more bum like the millions you saw on the road now.

She had gotten her job by a miracle, sitting over the last cup of coffee she could afford, loading it with sugar because that was the only food she would have all day, when the waitress behind the counter tore off her apron and told the diner's proprietor, "Sal, you're nothing but a cheap dago bastard," before hoofing it out the door.

Waitressing was all right. If you had nothing else to do with your life. Mr. Salvatore, who was close with a penny but otherwise not so bad, told her she'd rake in the tips, with gams like hers. But the days of the high-rolling tippers in Packards and Caddies were long gone. She didn't mind. She had two rooms, a roof over her head, and enough to eat. Money for the matinee once a week. She was rich, compared to the poor joes all over the streets.

An economic depression. Whatever you called it, it ruined men. And women, too. If in a different way. You saw it all the time. She didn't even expect tips anymore. Maybe a nickel now and then. Some poor buggers would leave a single penny. But that was all right. It was better than the fancy dressed men who still came in new cars, if less expensive ones, and ordered more than they could finish, then left a dime between four of them. The ten-cent-tip trade. Cheapskates who used hard times as an excuse to shortchange everybody else. You could talk all you wanted about bank failures, she had yet to see a banker starve to death.

The joe who had just lost his girl came back in with a paper bag under his arm. Wet. Him and the bag both.

"I think there's something in here," he said. More slump-shouldered than ever. "I don't know."

He dropped the bag on the counter and sat down. Too close to the cash register for Betty's comfort. Though he didn't look like he had the heart left to steal a pack of gum.

"I guess, I was her," he said abruptly, "I would've give up on me, too."

She decided to change the baby on a tabletop. Where she could keep an eye on the guy. Her last customer of the night. Merry Christmas, she thought bitterly.

"My own brother," he said. His anger was sudden, but weak and drained: the anger left at the bottom of life's cup. "Can you believe it, though? I figured I could count on my own brother. Took her up with me to Mahanoy City. For Christmas. Figured we could at least stay warm and feed ourselves up a little. My own brother wouldn't let us in the door. My own brother. Ain't that a kicker, Christmas Eve? No room at the inn, I guess. Not that I believe all that religion malarkey, I don't mean. That's all bushwa. But my own brother, just closing the door in my face like that. And him with a good job, besides. Acourse, his wife's always had her snoot in the air. She never liked me one bit. Called me a good-for-nothing red."

Betty worked on the infant. A boy, all right. Dirty as could be. What kind of mother was that little bum?

Betty could not understand, not in a million years and a day, how any mother could just walk out on her own baby like that. No matter how busted she was.

"Well, you sound like a red to me. Are you?" Betty asked, positioning the infant's bottom on the single clean diaper left in the bag.

"And if I was? What's it to you, sister?"

"I could care less. It doesn't make any difference to me. I was just asking to pass the time." The tabletop was going to need a good scrubbing. The baby did, too. How could a mother let her own kid go like that?

"It ought to make a difference. You're a worker, too. When the revolution comes, you won't have to live off tips anymore, off the crumbs of the rich and the bushwas."

Betty rose from her labor with the infant and put one hand on her hip. "Well, I guess the revolution's here, then. 'Cause I sure ain't living off tips. And I didn't see any rich guys in here shedding any crumbs lately, either."

"It isn't funny, sister. Working men and women have to stand together. The workers of the world are strong together. Look at Russia."

"You look at Russia. I'm glad to have a job in Reading, Pennsylvania."

"The Soviet Union is building a workers' paradise."

"Yeah? Well, you call me when it's ready. I'll give you my number." Even the safety pins were crusted. It was a disgrace. Betty knew she would never have let her own child go like that. "That why the steel mill let you go? Because you were a red?"

"Well, it wasn't because I was lazy. I'm proud to be a worker. There's dignity in work. In hard work. Physical work.

More than there is in an office job. Exploiting the masses. That's what the rich don't understand."

Betty had no interest in politics and such nonsense. All she knew about the reds from her years in Coaldale was that they talked the miners into going out on strike until the miners' families were starving and coughing up their lungs. Then the bosses came back with an offer of lower wage scales and the reds slipped away during the night, the ones that weren't beat up or killed.

"Here," she said. "You got to hold him now. I got to clean up that mess." She shook her head. "I'd be out on my Royal Canadian, Mr. Salvatore saw a mess like that on the top of a table."

"When this country turns Communist, he won't be able to fire you. The means of production are going to belong to everybody, not just the rich. Your boss is just a capitalist exploiter of the working class. In the future, he's going to have to work. Just like everybody else."

"Old Sal works hard already. I'll say that for him. Though young Sal's not worth much." She thought, earnestly, for a few seconds. "Really, the old guy ain't so bad. He doesn't give me no trouble, like some men would. He's a good family man, just off the boat himself. Half a dozen kids."

"The family is a bushwa institution. When the workers—"

"You just hold the kid while the working class cleans up this mess, all right?"

"You should be with us, comrade. It's not some kind of joke. We're fighting for you, too."

She paused. Staring at him. At the pathetic, dreary sight of him. "My name's 'Betty.' Not 'comrade.' Okay? And I think Mr. Roosevelt's doing the best he can, that's what I think."

"He's just a wolf in sheep's clothing, your Roosevelt! Look it. He's rich himself. His whole family's rich." He made a face like he just smelled the dirty diaper. "You think he cares about the workers of the world, your Roosevelt? Did he fight for the blue eagle? Did he? It's all nothing but a sham, a put-up job, all of it. The rich trying to put one over on the workingman, to keep us all quiet." He shook his head bitterly. "You think Roosevelt's out in the cold tonight, worrying about where he's going to sleep?"

She gathered up the soiled diaper, unsure what to do with it. It seemed foolish to throw it away. The baby was going to need it. She would have taken it into the ladies' to empty it, at least. But she had to keep her eye on the till. Red was bad enough. She didn't need him red-handed, too.

Without any warning, the guy began to cry. Just bawling like a kid. Betty took the baby off him again, setting the diaper on the floor by the counter.

"She must've gone with that trucker. I'll bet. You knew he was a bum. You saw through him. She must've gone with that truck driver."

He wasn't exactly a fast thinker, Betty told herself.

"I can't blame her," he went on, pathetic. "How can I blame her? When a workingman can't even put a roof over his girl's head for the night? When all the dough he got on him is barely enough for one last meal for her, and the only bunk he can offer her and her kid is the seat in his automobile? On Christmas Eve?" His head hung down. "I didn't even have the gas to get us to Philly. This is it. End of the line."

"What's in Philly that's so hot?"

He shook his head, sniffling like a kid who didn't have the sense to wipe his nose. "Pal of mine. I thought, maybe . . ."

He stopped speaking and collapsed back into sobs.

Smitty came out from the back. He made her jump. But he didn't notice his effect on her, she didn't think. He'd been asleep and was still groggy. Headed for the toilet.

"What's going on?" he demanded. Rubbing one eye, then the other. "Who's that bum? What's wrong with him?"

"He's just down on his luck," Betty said.

"Ain't we all. Cripes, Betty. You ain't been giving free handouts again, have you? Sal's going to—"

"I pay my way, mister," the guy said. He began to reach into his pocket.

"He already paid," Betty said. "If it matters so much to you. What's it to you, anyway?"

"I'm just trying to look out for you, for cripes sake. For the both of us. Jeez, you want us both out on the street? Like you ain't got it good here."

"Go on with you. It's time to close up, anyway."

Smitty scratched his gut under his apron, brushed by the Christmas tree, and disappeared through the swing door. He didn't wash his hands, ever. Betty knew that much.

"You're closing up?" the guy asked.

"Well, we got to close sometime. It's almost midnight,

buddy. And we ain't exactly breaking the bank with business. As you can see."

He nodded. "I got no place to go." He said it as guilelessly as a child might, with all the red talk and swagger cried out of him.

Betty handed back the infant, now that the guy's crying fit was over. "Neither does the baby, I suppose? I guess you don't know where to find his mother? Or his grandmother? Or anybody that gives two cents about him?"

"I don't even know if I know her real name. Margie's, I mean. She goes by Margaret Starr. But that never sounded right to me. Too hoity-toity, you know? She was on the stage in Philly. I figured maybe it was one of those stage names."

"She was on the stage? When you met her?"

"No. A while ago. She told me about it."

"Yeah. I bet I know what kind of stage she was on."

"Oh, lay off, would you? She's just a mixed-up kid. A victim of . . . of the capitalist system."

"And you're stuck with the baby."

He shrugged, unable to meet her eyes. "I guess I can give it to a home. They'll take it, won't they? The priests or somebody?"

"I thought you reds didn't believe in religion? Ain't there some Communist orphanage you can take him to?"

"Sister . . ." His face looked broken to bits, dead, and she was instantly sorry for needling him. ". . . if you were in my shoes . . ."

"I didn't mean nothing. Forget it, buddy. But what kind of life's a kid going to have in one of those homes? You ever heard what they're like?"

"It's better than being on the bum for a kid." Then he started thinking about something else, she could tell. "I guess I'll have to sell the car. Whatever I can get for it—you want to buy a car? It runs okay."

"Do I look like I got money for a car?" In fact, she just might have had enough saved to buy the car off him. If he was selling it cheap. But she didn't need or want a car. And buying his automobile would have spoiled things. Everything that was going to happen. "Look . . . if you promise to behave yourself, I can let you sleep in my front room. I got two rooms, with an outside entrance. But you'd have to be quiet . . ."

His face came back to life, the way a kid's did when he saw his Christmas stocking.

". . . and no funny business," she warned him. "I don't mean nothing but what I said. You can sleep in the front room, and nowhere else. For the kid's sake, I'm doing it." Then something collapsed inside her. Or outside of her. It was hard to tell exactly. She was like an eggshell breaking inward. But she was determined not to start crying in front of the guy. Or in front of anybody else.

"You listen to me good," she told him, hard-faced and determined. "No funny business. I mean it. I keep a thirty-two in the night table," she lied, "and I know how to use it."

"I'll do anything you say," he told her.

She looked at him, judging him one last time. But she knew him. She had known all she needed to know the first time she saw him. He was not going to disappoint her.

"Well, it's Christmas, ain't it?" she said. "Listen, when

Smitty comes back out—if he ever comes back out, I'm telling you—you take the kid there and get in your car and drive down the street. Drive down that way and wait around the corner while we close up. I don't want any talk."

"Shouldn't the baby stay in here where it's warm? I could go ahead and—"

"And how do you think that would look? Me here, with your baby?"

"I wasn't thinking."

The door to the gents' clapped shut and the swinging door pushed open. Smitty stumbled slightly as he came out. Hitting the sauce back in the kitchen again. Well, tomorrow, at least, he could sleep it off, as long as it took. He set the Christmas tree shaking. The glass balls glittered.

"Time to close up," Smitty said, testing his day-old beard with his fingers. "What're you doing, Bett? Writing a book with this guy or something?"

"Oh, I could write a book," she said. "Let me tell you."

As he rose to leave, with the infant in his arms, the guy eyed the thirty-five-cent tip the truck driver had left by the register. But he didn't touch it. He went out and started up his car.

She and Smitty had their routine down. Betty had already done most of the cleaning up and they were ready to go in fifteen minutes. They almost forgot to unplug the Christmas tree, though. And a fire was the last thing they all needed. Smitty had to unlock the door again so she could go in and disconnect the string of lights.

"Hey, kid," Smitty said, as he closed the door a second time. "I forgot my mistletoe. Want to just pretend?"

"Yeah. You wish."

He hadn't expected a kiss, or anything else. He just liked to razz her. And she liked to razz him back. They got along okay, to tell the truth. And Smitty knew when to close the other eye. Sometimes, for all his yelling, she wondered if Old Sal didn't know when to close an eye himself. You couldn't just let people starve.

"You ain't so bad, you know that?" Smitty said abruptly. "I said that first day, I said to Sal, you ain't so bad." He stood there, a fat old man who wasn't really old, a man without a family or any friends she knew of, and said, "Merry Christmas, Bett."

She almost smiled. "Merry Christmas, Smitty," she told him. Surprising herself, she gave him a peck on the cheek. Then she hurried off down the street in her galoshes, afraid the man and baby would be gone, afraid that she had been wrong about everything, and that she, too, would remain alone.

She never learned the guy's name. She didn't want to know it. He was as good as his word, that was all that mattered. He stayed in the front room, a big man sprawled over the end of a cast-off parlor sofa, with the infant bedded down in the clothes basket beside him. When the baby cried, hungry, lonely, in the middle of the night, Betty remained stern, staying under her covers, not because she was afraid of the man and the foolishness of men, but because she knew exactly how it had to be, how it was all going to work, and she did not want to spoil it.

She woke while it was still dark. Just after five, she could read the radium dial on the alarm clock. But she didn't move a muscle. She wouldn't even get up to go out to the bathroom, though she wanted to badly enough. She waited until she heard the man whose name she didn't know get up and move around. She believed she heard him going through the purse she had left lying by the door on purpose. She had even slipped in a few extra bucks from her savings, enough to get him at least as far as Philly. Then she heard him go out, trying hard not to make any noise, quiet as a gypsy when he clicked the door shut.

She waited a little longer. And waited. Until she imagined she heard a car start up down the street, where she had made him park before they sneaked up the outside stairs to her rooms. She thought she heard the car drive off. But she waited a last couple of minutes. In case he had forgotten anything. In case he would be foolish enough to return and spoil everything.

Finally, she got up and pulled her robe over her nightgown. It was cold. She could not find her slippers, couldn't remember where she put them.

Suddenly, her discipline collapsed. She rushed into the front room.

When she saw the baby lying in the clothes basket, still asleep, but moving—moving little fingers, an arm, a covered leg—she broke down and cried. Worse than the guy had bawled the night before. Much worse.

As she lifted the baby from its bed, he began to cry, too. But not for long. Then the early church bells began to peal, and Betty went to the window with the infant, to look out at the first gray light of Christmas.

The Day After Christmas

The day after Christmas the local mall
Opens its doors at eight.
Faithful shoppers crowd the stores
In a cold, acquisitive state.

Clothes are discounted forty percent
And seasonal items by half.
The hands are quick, the eyes are fierce,
And you will not hear a laugh.

Oh, a bargain is a marvelous thing!
A bargain swells the heart!
You return to your car with both arms full
And your soul in a shopping cart.

But the greatest bargain of all time
Was offered on Christmas morn,
In Palestine.

The Lie of the Land

✸

Christmas, 1960

There was no snow that year. Blue lights still lit the spruce trees in our yard, but the holiday turned its back and crowded indoors. Relatives appeared, bearing slight gifts. They fidgeted in the good chairs by the tree, eager for the envelopes of cash my father dispensed. Other adults, unseen throughout the year, dropped by for a holiday drink, thrusting their children upon us. The children were as unhappy to visit as we were to receive them, but my little brother, even at five, always made the best of his misfortunes. He was a lovely child, which I was not.

I caught one boy stealing a miniature car, but the grown-ups laughed it off.

Our visitors must have been disappointed by the meager alcohol on offer. They knew my father as a generous man and a warm, capacious drinker. But our home held only two bottles, one each of Haig & Haig and Canadian Club, and only at

Christmas. The liquor stayed out of sight, under the sink. My mother retained that single Methodist prejudice.

Of course, there were bottles for gifts and for the mailman, but those didn't count.

We had a fine Nativity scene, displayed amid the presents, then ignored. The reek of pine, not faith, lifted our hearts. The usual kitchen scents of coffee and cigarettes hid below the fumes of holiday baking, which grew denser every day: burning sugar, the bitterness of walnuts, hot raisins, and the sour smell of dough. Cinammon, ginger, and cloves.

Life grew abundant. All the lights stayed on.

My aunt Mariah, who never married, made cheesecakes by a recipe from Lindy's in New York, a city as far away and bright as Bethlehem. The cheesecakes were tart and not for me. Thin and brittle, her gingerbread men were never as good as they smelled. Their buttons hurt my teeth, which were bad that year, making room for their betters. My mother made potato candy, my favorite. Each bite shocked down through nerve and gum, but I ate all I could stuff in, grabbing the biggest slices from between wax-paper layers, spirals of peanut butter over-whelmed by sugar paste chilled almost to freezing.

And then there was ribbon candy, which I never liked but my father loved, telling us over and over how it had been the treat of his childhood, impossibly long before. My brother liked it, too, and cut his lip on a sliver. My mother wanted to ban it from the house thereafter, but my father bought big boxes of it anyway.

If you put "*O Tannenbaum*" on the record player, tears filled my father's eyes. His fists were as big as coal shovels. When he was young, real candles lit the Christmas trees, and houses burned down because a child was careless. I would have liked real candles on our tree. But my father had all the say in trimming it, a ritual during which my brother and I played regulated parts. My mother took no interest until we finished.

My father would hang the hand-painted balls from Germany, sailors with accordions, blue flowers on white oblongs, gold stars, and rainbow spangles. Icicles of glass. My father was a huge man, strong and fat, a good dancer, light of touch, and sometimes frightening. My brother and I threw the tinsel, as high as we could, to finish the job. My father made a final rearrangement.

There were candy canes, too, but I don't recall anyone eating them or even taking them out of their cellophane. We were supposed to have them, so we did. Everyone, except my aunt Mariah, who liked sour things and had worse teeth than me, preferred the chocolates from Moota's, butter creams, caramels, and nuts. A two-pound box disappeared overnight, as if thieves had come among us.

My brother ate cone-shaped chocolate pops, shedding brown flakes on the carpet.

We knew about some of the toys that had been bought for us. They were the ones I wanted, which I had convinced my brother to ask for, as well. We did not believe in Santa Claus. We believed in my father. I spared, at most, a random thought for the Christ child, although I liked the story well enough. The black king near the manger made me wonder. The Negro help at the New Jersey shore were not that sort at all.

When the grown-ups raised their voices now, no anger came between them. Aunt Mariah's snicker approached a laugh. Visitors crowded the kitchen after dinner, unless we had gone shopping for the evening. I had a formidable list of gifts to buy for others, but first I bought King's Men cologne for my father and cuff links, too, from the bargain table at Pomeroy's. I chose gifts with great care, squeezing an immensity from my five allotted dollars. I cannot recall the gift I bought my mother that year.

The telephone call came two nights before Christmas. It broke the gorgeous pattern of the days.

Memory plays favorites. I could not say what was baking that evening, or what my brother and I were eating off our trays as we watched *The Early Show* from Philadelphia. But I do recall Errol Flynn as Robin Hood. In black and white, of course. Even then, I knew Maid Marian wouldn't hold him. It was the same with *Captain Blood,* a film I had seen as many times and liked a good deal better. Errol Flynn was my hero. He was always lunging about, dashing and smiling. Even chained to a galley's oars or thrust into a dungeon, he knew he couldn't lose for very long. He was like my father that way, although my father was big enough to make four of him. The woman—Olivia de Havilland in both movies—was too weak. He was bound to exceed her.

I understood so much, and grasped so little. At eight, I had a crush on Ava Gardner. I could not have given a solid reason why. I had more sense of the world than I could manage.

The phone rang. Aunt Mariah went to answer. I could not have heard her voice from the den where the television sat. But her tone would have been accusatory, as always. No salesman at the door ever got past her. The milkman had learned not to question a missing empty.

I *did* hear her call out my mother's name: Rose. Perhaps it's only the way we remember things, forcing them into sequence, but I believe that syllable was enough to warn me that something unwanted had happened.

It was too early for visitors on a weeknight, even at Christmas. You didn't come during dinner, that was a rule. And my father wasn't home yet. We were alone, incomplete.

My mother ran to the phone. Not long after, Aunt Mariah appeared in the doorway, face as nasty as the Sheriff of Nottingham's.

"What are you two up to?" she demanded.

We weren't up to anything. Aunt Mariah turned away before I could say a word in our defense.

I always spoke for my brother.

I followed Aunt Mariah back through the kitchen. My mother stood at the phone in the hallway, crying. Her fingers smeared her face.

"Calm down and tell me what happened, would you?" she demanded, although she wasn't calm herself. "Just tell me what happened and stop your silly nonsense."

"What's the matter?" I asked my aunt Mariah, who stood between us.

"Just you go back to the den," she said. "It's none of your business."

I went back to the den but found a series of excuses to return to the kitchen, to look down the hall, to listen. My mother phoned one place after another, trying to find my father. Sometimes, he had to work late at his colliery, even at Christmas. Or he had to meet people. Contractors and surveyors. The men from Philadelphia who always stayed at the Necho Allen. Most of them had to do with coal, but some only talked about horses.

I even knew the places where my father went: Scraffords. Taylor's Diner. The Pottsville Club, where children were not welcome, not even my father's children. Sometimes he went to Hazleton, to Stan Gennetti's or Gus Gennetti's, or all the way to Wilkes-Barre—although Wilkes-Barre meant the bank and hours of daylight. In the summer, I spent whole days with him. Visiting those places. He was proud of me. He bought me books. While I waited, I read them in the lobbies or sitting with the bookkeepers in the colliery office.

"Is Dad all right?" I asked. My alarm was as disabling as a toothache.

"It's not about your father. Go back to the den," Aunt Mariah told me. "It doesn't concern you."

"Can we turn the tree lights on yet?"

My mother went off in her car. She had a white Cadillac then, and my father drove a black one. They were regal automobiles, although I could not have used such a word in those days.

Aunt Mariah stayed with my brother and me. She didn't quite cry. She smoked her Salem cigarettes and neglected the dirty dishes.

When my father came in, she shouted at him. In a voice my mother never would have used. Almost a scream, it made my brother look at me. He had an eager, expectant face, too trusting. Like the softest of my mother's relatives. Even when he was afraid, you would have thought he was waiting for an ice-cream cone.

"What the hell's the matter with you?" my father bellowed. He filled chairs, car seats, doorways, entire rooms, buildings, landscapes, horizons. His voice could be heard above the noise of a coal breaker, above slamming mine cars. In restaurants, men's eyes went right to him, instead of searching out the pretty girls. He always seemed impatient for the world to catch up to him, to stop wasting his time, to just hand over what he wanted and be done with it.

My aunt nodded past him to where I stood. I wonder how she spotted me behind the bulk of him. I remember my father as bulldozers and dollars in the fist, with a face carved from a side of raw beef and heavy gabardine shirts buttoned up beneath his suit jacket. He wore galoshes for the coal yards but would not wear an overcoat, although he owned several. I never saw him in a pair of gloves. He was stronger than the weather.

He looked back toward me, glasses still half-clouded from the cold outside. I couldn't quite see his eyes.

"Go back in the den and shut the door."

His voice was iron. I stepped back and shut the door, but put my ear to the wood, the way Lucille Ball did on television. I could not hear enough to understand. My father's voice grew unusually quiet, while my aunt Mariah seemed ready to start shouting again, but kept stopping herself. I heard her say, "the bum, that little tramp."

My father went back outside and started his car.

Uncle Ivor was dead. Nobody told me. But by the next morning, I knew. My mother had almost stopped crying. She didn't smoke, but drank cup after cup of coffee. My father hardly said a word, but his silence had a growl in it. I had intended to ask if my brother and I could each open just one present, since it was already the day before Christmas. But I was afraid of my father's temper now. It did not burst over us often, but when it did the heavens fell.

I ate my cereal in front of the TV set. The talk in the kitchen was like a car that wouldn't start, no matter who turned the key. Snooping, I heard my father tell Aunt Mariah, "Just keep that dirty mouth of yours to yourself. You don't know what you're talking about."

"And I suppose you do?" my aunt Mariah answered back. She wasn't afraid of my father. She was the only one. Sometimes I thought she wanted him to hit her. "Well, we know that's shit for the birds. Don't we?"

We drove over to Coaldale that morning, leaving Aunt Mariah to mind my brother. My father said she should come along, with Billy, that the whole family should go, but Aunt

Mariah said she wouldn't so much as look at the little bum, that she wouldn't go near her.

"Who's a bum?" I asked.

"You watch your mouth," my mother said, "and go out and get in the car." She had gathered up the presents for Uncle Ivor's kids. It looked like too many to me. I was supposed to go along to play with Randy and Christine, to cheer them up, but they were dull and always needed bossing.

I took along a comic book about the Vikings, a thick one that cost twenty-five cents. But I'd read it too many times. And my father turned off the radio in the middle of a carol. It was easier to read when my parents talked or at least played the radio. The silence was like having a stranger in the car with us.

We drove up the valley, through a world I already knew as I would never know another in my lifetime. When there was snow, whiteness covered the black banks and the coal-dirt shabbiness of the towns. But there was no snow that year and it looked just like any other day, except where the Hunkies had covered their houses with lights and filled their tiny yards with Santa's reindeer. Even as a child I knew it wasn't the way we did things, that it wasn't right, that riot of decoration. Blue lights draped on two spruce trees reached the limit.

We passed through Cumbola. The day was as gray as dust. I knew the names of the long string of collieries as well as I knew the names of the towns and patches. Maybe half were working that day, at least until noon, filling the Reading Railroad cars on the sidings. I knew the different kinds of coal, from rice to buck, and the acid scent of breakers, the smeared faces of the miners at the shift's end. The old-timers still lugged their pit meal in deckers, while younger men carried lunch buckets, just like the Dutchies from the aluminum plant. But a man who worked in a mill was nothing compared to an anthracite miner.

I could have told you the difference between a shaft and a slope mine, between gangways and galleries. The Sally K colliery, which once had been my father's, had a Santa perched on the roofbeam, as if climbing into the coal hoppers with his bag. My father's new breaker, up the road, was bigger. Electric candles lit his office windows and there was a wreath on the door the truckers used. His colliery was closed for Christmas Eve, and the day was so drab you could see the lamplight down in the watchman's shanty. Then we entered Tamaqua, with decorations strung above the street and last-minute shoppers plunging between parked cars. Despite my parents' silence, it felt like Christmas again.

I didn't know, of course, that we were teetering on a ledge and losing our balance. King Coal was dying, almost dead. Half of those storefronts would stand empty in ten years, with the last collieries abandoned. I wonder now how much my father saw and refused to admit to himself. He built his dream as wiser men dismantled his world. Foolhardy, confident that luck couldn't resist him, he believed there would always be more than there had been.

"The roads were dry," my mother said abruptly. "It was still daylight."

The red light at Five Points had stopped us. It was one of

the few things that could have stopped my father. He drove his black Cadillac as fast as he wanted to and the police knew they weren't supposed to bother him.

"He was drunk," my father snapped. "Don't be a fool."

Lately, there had been arguments about papers my mother needed to sign, about money in her name that my father said wasn't hers and never had been hers, but the bickering seemed to have stopped for Christmas. Now his voice was hard, though he did not raise it.

"Ivor wasn't a drinker," my mother said. The light turned green. "Ivor was never a drinker. Why would he leave work in the middle of the day? You tell me that."

"He was a drinker yesterday. Ask the state cops."

"Ivor *wasn't* a drinker. And why would he leave work? Why didn't you stop him? Couldn't you have stopped him, Paul? He always listened to you. . . ."

My father's big fist tightened on the steering wheel. "Stop talking like a crazy woman. Cripes, you should hear yourself talk. You should just hear yourself. I wasn't even there yesterday, and I told you that. I was up trying to get that bugger Kruno to pay his bills. In Hazleton."

"Dottie was there. *She* should've stopped him. Ivor was never drunk a day in his life. He must've heard something." She glanced back toward me, the way grown-ups do. "You know what I mean."

My father ignored her gesture. His voice hardened with disgust. "What's the matter with you, for God's sake? Can't you all face a fact? Ivor was drunk and he drove his car into a strip-

ping pit. It was his fault and nobody else's. No matter what anybody else did or didn't do. *His* fault. Period. Merry Christmas."

"She drove him to it," my mother said, in that quiet voice
more determined than any rage. My father did not reply.

We drove past Wenzel's bakery, where we would have
stopped to buy sticky buns on a better day. Instead, we went
over the hill to the patch where my mother's family hailed from,
where my grandfather still lived in half a company house across
from the silt banks. The house had new siding my father had
paid for. He had bought the house outright for Pop, for three
thousand dollars, when the LC&N put it up for sale. And I
knew he gave my grandfather enough money to pay his tab at
the Greenwood Inn, where the old miners drank and coughed.

My grandfather slipped me quarters and Hershey Bars, always wearing his little Welsh grin, as if he and I shared secrets.
In the summer, there was strawberry milk in the refrigerator,
which Pop still called an icebox. My grandfather was small and
seemed terribly old. I realize now that he could not have been
much older than my father.

There was no Hershey Bar that day. There should have
been a Christmas gift for me, but if there was, Pop forgot to
bring it down from upstairs. Somehow, I had the sense not to
inquire.

The parlor air was brown. It was always brown, summer
and winter.

There was no tree, although Pop usually put up a small one.
Perhaps he had taken it down since the day before. He sat in his

chair between the new television and the old radio set, which was bigger than the TV. He didn't say a word, just turned his head now and then, as if he were going to speak but couldn't find any words in his pocket.

Aunt Dottie was with him, without her husband or her son, who was grown and in college and wanted no part of his relatives. Aunt Dottie was the eldest of Pop's children, the eldest and the strongest, the one who had made it out of the patch on her own. She was generous with everyone in her family, but every generosity worried her. She always gave what was needed, but it pained her. As if she knew she had to keep on saving desperately, that her family was a magnet for disaster.

"You go over, if you want," Aunt Dottie said, bitter as medicine. "I'd just slap that makeup and lipstick right off her face. Her all dolled up like a you-know-what, in the middle of the day. And Ivor working like a dog for her." She looked up toward my mother, then toward my father and back to Pop. "We all told him not to marry one of them. *I* told him. A thousand times. I *begged* him. They all run around, every one of them. I told him, but would he ever listen?"

I put two and two together. They were talking about my aunt Helena. Her family was Lithuanian and she was Roman Catholic, neither of which were good things for anyone to be. Aunt Helena and Uncle Ivor had been married as long as I could remember, and the talk had always been there. Whenever I heard my mother and Aunt Mariah talk about her "running around," I pictured Aunt Helena running madly through the streets of Coaldale. It made no sense, since she was always so still, so quiet, so careful of things, and politer than anyone in my mother's family. But she only gave you half a soda in the summertime, and their refrigerator was never full.

I liked Aunt Helena. I knew my mother was young and pretty, because everybody said so and made a fuss over her in front of my father. But Aunt Helena was the kind of pretty that made me want to sit close to her and find a reason to touch her. Her hair was as black as shoe polish. She was friendly, in a calm way, never silly. Looking back, I would describe her as solemn, even tragic. But such matters were not yet part of my experience.

Uncle Ivor had been the silly one, always smiling when he was around her. He had a grin like someone in a comic book, that big. My mother said Aunt Helena wore too much perfume, and that it was cheap stuff she bought off the peddler. But I liked it.

Aunt Helena had the perfect white skin and rose-petal lips I later would read about in Victorian novels. The truth is that I would have liked to kiss her.

"Well, I'm not going to let her sit there all alone, with those two kids on her hands and her husband dead," my father told us. "Come on, Paulie." He stood up, tugging the world with him. I was already reaching for my coat.

"Let her Hunkie relations drive down and sit with her. Let *them* sit with her," my aunt Dottie said.

"Rose?" my father said. "Are you coming, or not?"

My mother got her purse from Pop's kitchen table.

"Sure you don't want to come, Dot?" she asked as she paused in the closeness of the parlor. "We won't stay long."

"I'd tell her she could go to Hell and rot," my aunt Dottie said. She did not see me, although I stood right in front of her. "Reese, Lewis . . . now Ivor." She reached her hand toward Pop's knee, but withdrew it before she touched him.

I knew about Uncle Reese. He had been wounded by the Germans and came home to die. Uncle Lewis went with the TB before I was born. Everyone spoke of him with special affection. They said he could have been a professional dancer.

Pop just sat, saying nothing. Not even, "So long, champ," or "Merry Christmas."

We drove past the inn and our little Methodist church, then up Kline's Hill into Coaldale. Aunt Helena and Uncle Ivor didn't live in a house of their own. They had an apartment above a garage, along past the Miner's Hospital and the high school. The apartment was small and always smelled of cooking. Their children had dull toys.

Uncle Ivor had worked for my father, aboveground in the boiler plant. His lungs were too weak for the mines. No taller than his wife, or not much, he always seemed as if he had just let something slip from his hand. Sometimes, just after payday, he would give me a nickel and tell me, "Don't spend it all in one place."

You had to climb outside stairs to get to the apartment. It was good that there had been no snow, because ice got on the steps. A man from the bank had broken his leg the year before and my father had to pay off a loan for Ivor.

Oh, I knew far more than my parents realized I did. But not as much as I thought.

My mother knocked, then my father just went inside. There was an aluminum tree in a corner of the tiny living room, with solid-colored balls on its branches, the kind on sale at the grocery store. A few packages lay underneath the tree. I wondered if any were mine. Uncle Ivor never gave good presents. But any present was better than none.

Randy and Christine weren't there, I could tell instantly.

A man's voice called, "Hello, hello!"

It was my uncle Dai. He was a Williams, not a Roberts. He had been sitting in the kitchen with Aunt Helena. Uncle Dai was a miner, but you never would have guessed it. He dressed up, and his clothes were always as perfect as those worn by snooty Englishmen on TV shows. He had a little mustache, exactly like Errol Flynn's, and my mother said he got manicures. He wasn't married and he didn't like kids, but he always acted glad to see me for the first few minutes. My father had paid off a man in Mahanoy City so he wouldn't give Uncle Dai a beating, but my aunt Mariah said a beating would have been good for him.

"Merry Christmas," Uncle Dai went on, "*Merry* Christmas." It was as if he couldn't think of anything else to say, almost as if something scared him. At the sight of my father and mother, he had jumped to his feet.

Abruptly, he changed his tone and added, "Well, not that's it's all that merry this year, I suppose. Not the best of Christmases this one, is it? Poor, old Ivor."

Aunt Helena sat still, as if we were ghosts she couldn't see and didn't hear. Uncle Dai put his hand on her shoulder. She wore a white blouse. His hand was pink and clean.

"You buck up, Helena," Uncle Dai said. "You just buck up. Everything's going to be all right, and that's a promise."

"Get out, Dai," my father said, in a voice that didn't bother to be angry. "Or I'll throw you down those stairs myself."

Uncle Dai's hand leapt from Aunt Helena's shoulder. My father had been a county-fair prizefighter when he was a young miner. He had been in jail, too, during Prohibition. He laughed about it and told a story about the warden's daughter that I didn't understand completely. But I understood about Prohibition because of *The Untouchables* on TV. My father used to watch the show and laugh. The odd thing, looking back, is that he always rooted for Eliot Ness.

He had tattoos all over. He tried to teach me how to box, but failed.

"I was just going, that's the truth of it," Uncle Dai said. His voice quivered and he did not quite look at my father. "Just paying my respects, Paul. You understand. Just paying my respects."

There were vast gaps in what I knew, but I could tell that Uncle Dai had no real part in what was going on around me. He was a fly that had been whisked away. He picked up his hat and his velvet-collared topcoat from the back of a chair, then fled. I heard him running down the outside steps. My father unclenched his fists.

"Don't let him back in this house," my mother told Aunt

Helena. "You know all he's interested in, I don't have to tell you." Then she looked at me and held her peace.

Aunt Helena moved at last. Her face was changed, blotched, ugly enough to worry me. She looked up at my mother, who was younger, taller, and dressed like a woman on a magazine cover.

"I know," Aunt Helena said. "I know what you all think. I know what you all think about me. I know what you say. But I made him happy. You can't say I didn't make him happy."

She had a faint accent. It made her voice sound broken.

Aunt Helena began to weep. Crying hard. Flattening her face against the pale green tabletop. She made a fist, but only tapped the wood with it. My father took me out of the room, but I heard her say, "I want him back, I want him back, they can't take him. . . ."

My father gave me two dollars. He told me to go around the corner to the five-and-dime and come back in an hour. I was happy about that. I always liked to go off on my own. And this was Christmas Eve, the world held wonders.

I felt as if I had escaped a punishment. With Randy and Christine off somewhere, I would have had to sit there doing nothing, since Uncle Ivor's television set had been taken away. My father had been angry about that, telling my mother that Uncle Ivor was weak and shiftless, that he couldn't keep a dollar in his pocket.

I remembered.

🌺

My brother and I were up before light, ransacking our presents. My mother and father resisted the tumult as long as they could, but Aunt Mariah felt the pull of the kitchen and the coffeepot. She emerged from her bedroom smoking a cigarette.

I had no thought to spare for Uncle Ivor. It was Christmas. Besides, he hadn't been an important uncle. My attention was focused on the matching sets of Civil War soldiers my brother and I had received. I already owned several books about the Civil War—the new year would begin its centennial—and my excitement had spilled downward. Billy knew that the blue soldiers were the good guys, and he resisted being the Confederate commander. Later on, he would prove himself a born rebel, vivid and wild of soul. But, at five, he was gentle and amiable. He soon gave in. Battle lines stretched across the floor, our soldiers waiting to die in the holiday dawn.

My father came in to have a look, in his trousers and an undershirt—he wore the old-fashioned kind with straps and the top of a heart tattoo showed on his chest. He was smiling.

"Is that what you wanted?" he asked us. "Did you get everything you wanted? Paulie? Billy?"

"Merry Christmas, Dad."

He didn't get a hug. We were too busy.

He sat and watched us, and we soon forgot him. The smell of cooking bacon vanquished every scent in the house. Too soon, we were summoned to eat our breakfasts, although Billy and I had better things to do.

Everyone seemed normal. Christmas normal. The morning hours were infinite and quick at the same time. Tears came to my brother's eyes, when he saw how easily I had defeated his solid-gray army, but his resentments never lasted. The day outside was the color of Billy's troops.

"Get dressed, Paulie," my mother told me, coming around the corner with the suddenness to which I was accustomed. "Your father wants to take you over to church."

That meant a long ride to Coaldale, tedium, unbearably much of the holiday lost. We never went to church on Christmas Day. Never.

"Why? Do I *have* to?"

"Your father wants to take you." It was a formulation that allowed no further argument. As if she had said, "It's raining," during a thunderstorm. My father's desires were not proposals.

My father stepped into the room himself, putting his arm around my mother, as he would do less frequently in the years still left to him.

"You need to learn there's more to Christmas than toys," he said.

"Just be home in time for dinner, you," my mother told him. "You know the pack of them will be here waiting."

Billy wasn't forced to go along. It was just my father and me. That was better. I got to sit up front. Along the familiar route, the Hunkies had their decorations lit up in the daytime. My father played the radio. One carol after another. I knew the words, almost all of them. Before we reached Port Carbon, he was telling stories. I had heard them all before, but never tired of them. How Christmas had been a lean business in his child-hood, but his father always made sure there was a tree. How he had left school after the third grade to work as a breaker boy, and how each boy was given a little bag of gum candies, tied with a ribbon, as a Christmas gift from the foreman's wife. He did not speak of poverty or hardship in a tone of complaint, but in a voice of pride, of something akin to joy, as a hero might have told of dragons slain. His memories were a source of end-less fascination to him, and he felt compelled to hand them down to me.

In Tamaqua, the streets were empty, with even the cops gone home for Christmas dinner.

The little church at the edge of the patch, tan-shingled, al-ways made me think of the hymn about the "little brown church in the vale." It was just a chapel, really, small and unadorned, its interior one step above planks and trestles. We were Primi-tive Methodists, like my mother's family, who long had lived in the house closest to the church, with only the Greenwood Inn and a junkyard between their front door and God's.

Reverend Evans was always glad to see my father, who never forgot to put a big bill in the plate. My father had bought the church its first organ. That Christmas, the reverend acted as if it were a miracle to see us. He fawned, although my father always said he was a good man.

I had no idea then how poor they all were.

Reverend Evans, like my uncle Dai the day before, wished us "Merry Christmas," before recalling my uncle's death. Then his smile vanished and he slumped.

"Well, then, Mr. Ritter," he said to my father, "tomorrow, is it? With Father Coughlin presiding, I assume? A sad business, the wife persuading poor Ivor to follow the pope."

The church was scant of worshippers. Christmas Day was not given to religion, not even among Primitive Methodists. Later, I learned that my father had been raised a Lutheran, although his mother had been a German Catholic. He would have been well suited to our own times, since he seemed to find one church as good as another.

No one from my mother's family had come down to the service. I couldn't see into such matters then, but the women in that family had no use for God. They were of the earth, and resolutely so. It was the Parry men, flinty and small, who were God-bothered. But they died young, the most of them.

So it was always my father who took me to church on Sundays, sometimes sitting beside me, sometimes only dropping me off while he spent the hour elsewhere. But he always gave me money for the collection plate and told me to behave.

I was resigned to my fate that Christmas. And the service was not so bad. We sang familiar carols, instead of dreary hymns with endless verses. Reverend Evans told us that we all should be thankful and happy. As he spoke, I was.

My father did not sing along—he never did—but stood with the hymnal open in his hands. I followed along with my hand on his forearm, reading over the thickness of his fingers. But when we sat, he was different from other times. Despite the energy swelling him to bursting, he had the gift of sitting very still. The way you imagine kings sitting in storybooks. But that day he was restless on the hard wood of the pew, almost like the relatives who came to the house to collect their Christmas envelopes.

I was proud to be with my father, as I always was. As we waited in line to shake the reverend's hand, everyone came up to wish us a Merry Christmas. You might have mistaken my father for the preacher, the way they all crowded near him.

I thought we would go home then, or perhaps stop briefly at Pop's to drop off his envelope. Instead we turned up the hill toward Coaldale's heart.

"Where are we going *now*?" I complained. Although I swear I knew.

He parked down the street from Uncle Ivor's apartment. I hoped he would give me a dollar or two and tell me to come back later, even though I knew all the stores were closed. But he took me by the hand and led me up those stairs.

He knocked, then we went in immediately.

Randy and Christine were home, playing on the floor. I noted that Randy had been given a Civil War set just like mine and Billy's — my mother's doing, that would have been. Had I had that extra set myself, my brother and I could have staged much bigger battles.

Aunt Helena sat deep in an armchair. She was small and looked fragile, as if her bones would splinter at too hard a touch. Her face was almost pretty again, though swollen and red round the eyes. But her hair was unbrushed and she still wore yesterday's blouse, a thing my mother never would have done.

"Paul," she said, rising to face my father. Her tone was foreign to me. She didn't even wish me a Merry Christmas.

"You kids play," my father commanded. Wordlessly, Aunt Helena went into the kitchen. My father followed behind. A moment later, he drew the curtain that Uncle Ivor had instead of a door.

I was already planning to bring some toys along the next time we came, to trade with Randy for his Civil War soldiers. Christine was busy with a blond doll. She had light-brown hair and a narrow face, like Uncle Ivor, although Randy took after my aunt. I told Randy we should have a battle and I began to line up the soldiers.

He didn't say a word about his father.

Randy was the same age as me, but my brother knew more than he did. I was explaining how soldiers line up in rows to march, when my aunt Helena cried out.

We all stopped. Looking toward the kitchen. Christine's doll fell headfirst onto the carpet.

"I don't *want* it," Aunt Helena wailed. I had never heard a voice like that, though I would in the years to come. "Don't you understand that I can't take it?"

She sounded as if she were being hurt, but I saw my father through the crack in the curtains. He sat apart from her.

Randy stood up. Ready to run to his mother.

"Stay here," I ordered. I don't know why I did that. The words came instantly.

Randy had already learned the obedience the poor showed in those days. He sat back down, looking at me, then toward the kitchen, then back at me again. As if I had him on a leash. His little sister puckered toward tears.

My father stood up, parts of his big body flashing across the gap in the curtains. My aunt Helena sobbed.

"Don't be a horse's ass, Ellie," he told her. "You're going to need every penny, and you know it."

We left just after that. At first, my father was glum. But between Tamaqua and Newkirk, he tuned the radio back to the Pottsville station and asked if I wanted to sing along with the carols. We sang together for song after song, but he stopped singing long before I got tired of it. Then, while they were playing "Silver Bells," which made me think of trips to Philadelphia, I saw tears on his cheek.

Between Cumbola and the old roller rink at Dream City, there was a roadside lot where the coal trucks waited. It was empty now. My father pulled into it. The Cadillac bounced roughly until we stopped. With Bing Crosby singing the final verse, my father grasped me by the shoulders and pulled me against him.

My father knew how to hug in a way that left you in no doubt about his strength, yet never hurt. His hugs were invincibly firm—you would not escape—yet lavishly gentle. Looking back on things, I don't believe he learned that skill from hugging little boys.

As the radio advertised after-Christmas sales, my father took off his glasses and laid them on the dashboard. He wiped his face with one thick hand, loosening his grip on me.

"Things go wrong," he said. His voice was quiet, as if

telling me a secret. "You can't ever be afraid when things go wrong. Don't ever be afraid of anything, Paulie."

And he pulled back onto the road. Ours was the only car all the way to Port Carbon. It felt like Christmas, but in a strange sort of way. As we drove out of the last coal town, heading toward the clean place where we lived, my father turned down the radio.

"If your mother asks what took us so long," he told me, "tell her we stopped at Zizelmann's, to see about the funeral arrangements. Just tell her we stopped at the funeral home, if she asks. There's no need to worry her about things."

"Why would she be worried?"

"Just tell her we stopped at Zizelmann's, if she asks. Say you stayed in the car. And I'll get you another box of those soldiers."

But she didn't ask. The house was thick with the smells of turkey and ham, of bread stuffing and gravy, and of the Sunday-best of relatives come to call with mothballs still in their pockets. Some had liquor on their breaths, though most did not.

They knew they were not to stay for Christmas dinner, unless they had been invited in advance. But they all came to pay their respects. And to get their envelopes. For half an hour or so, Uncle Ivor was already forgotten. Then they left and we sat down to eat.

It was a good Christmas, after all. My brother and I got everything we wanted. And Billy and I did not have to go to the funeral the next day. We had a new babysitter who didn't bother us while we were playing and didn't make a fuss about being our friend. Billy and I re-created the Battle of Gettysburg, about which I had no more than an inkling, although I pretended otherwise. We ate leftovers for lunch, with cranberry sauce cold from the refrigerator, the way I liked it. We finished the pumpkin pie.

In the early afternoon, we had snow flurries. But they didn't amount to anything.

On Christmas Night

As I walked out on Christmas night
To drop the trash by the curb,
Heaven flamed in glory bright
Above our mild suburb.

Sleet had sizzled through the dawn
And snow fell until three,
Chastening the dormant lawns
Beneath the half-white trees.

We celebrated lovingly,
Welcoming the storm.
The world was locked beyond the wreath.
We were well-fed and warm.

Yet, timeless shadows crossed my heart
As darkness dimmed the land.
Men hate, as if He never came
To stay our killing hands.

They shout for war and warn of strife
In every tortured hour.
We live under the sinner's knife
In an age of heretic power.

But I walked out on Christmas night
To do a simple chore,
And Heaven flamed in glory bright
As it shall for evermore.